ETERNITY'S Edge

THE LOVE LEGACY
Book Three

A.F. VOYLES

aBM

Published by:
A Book's Mind
PO Box 272847
Fort Collins, CO 80527
www.abooksmind.com

Copyright © 2016
ISBN: 978-1-944255-63-3
Printed in the United States of America

No part of this publication may be reproduced, stored in a retrieval system, or transmitted in any form or by any means – electronic, mechanical, digital photocopy, recording, or any other without the prior permission of the author.

All rights reserved solely by the author. The author guarantees all contents are original and do not infringe upon the legal rights of any other person or work. The views expressed in this book are not necessarily those of the publisher.

My desire is that this series will bring hope to your heart and minister to your soul through creative writing and the inspiration of the Holy Spirit.

This book is dedicated to:

- The countless individuals who have fought the beast of fear in their lives and overcome, and to those who fight the battle every day.
- The many friends and sisters in Jesus who have uplifted me through their prayers and encouragement, who have stood with me during the darkest hours and the most brilliant of days. (Prov. 17:17 – A friend loves at all times. Prov. 18:24 - A friend sticks closer than a brother. NJK)
- The valiant warriors who stand in the gap for others.
- All who have faced and fought the battle of cancer, including my sister, Rose. We love you! You are a fighter and Overcomer!

Thank you to my hero and the bravest man I know, Melvin (Red) Voyles, my husband, lover and friend. Thank you for the sacrifices you have made and continue to make to see my dreams come true. Thank you for being my biggest cheerleader and my dearest friend. May Yahshua (Jesus) fulfill your hearts desires and make all your dreams come true.

Thank you to all the individuals who have been a positive influence and spoken into my life. Thank you to my family (blood born and blood bought)! I love you all! Thank you to my brother Larry for teaching me more than you will ever realize. I hope one day you will see what I see in you.

Thank you to my publisher – Jenene Scott, Floyd (A Book's Mind Team), and Christine Flower (editor) for your tireless effort and unyielding patience with me to make my books all they can be and pushing me to greater heights.

Thank you most of all to my precious Heavenly Father, Abba (Daddy), for planting in me Your seed of creativity through your son, Yahshua (Jesus Christ). Thank you for empowering me by Your Holy

Spirit to do all that you call me to do. Thank you for the light of Your revelation shining through this story and allowing Your life to come forth Your way. Nothing is impossible with You!

Chapter One
THE HEAVENLIES

Aaron walked along the white sand, waves cresting the salty air with the smell of freshness like that of newly formed snow. His grasp held the palm of his little three-year-old granddaughter, Angel, her miniature fingers wrapped around his tanned hand. The seagulls thrust their squawking voices like a ball being volleyed back and forth. It's as if the pesky birds were following them as they walked, skipped, and laughed along the silken smooth seashore.

Angel's tight curls bounced in the wind. She was a fraction in comparison to her grandpa's size. His pockets carried their bounty collected from the beach. The shells were a mixture of mollusk, conchology, and snail. The colors were silver, pink and pearl, beautiful in splendor. As Aaron held a shell to her ear the soothing nature tantalized the little girl. Angel's brown eyes grew wide with excitement. She jumped up and down. Aaron watched with sheer joy as she chased the waves back and forth shrilling as the water nearly engulfed her pink clogs. It made him thankful for every moment.

"Five minutes, Sweetie, we need to go; not too close. The water is still cold. Brrr," Aaron cautioned pretending to shiver.

Aaron scooped the child up in his arms and hugged her tight. Then lifted her on top of his shoulders, and she cackled with glee. He sang the song of "Puff the Magic Dragon," as they made their way back to the bungalow. They had rented for this special vacation celebrating the remission of cancer that wrecked his body the previous years. He never thought he would have this precious time with his loved ones.

"Papa! Papa!" a little voice yelled above the crashing waves. "Look!" Her hand pulled on his head to turn it toward the water. Out in the distance a school of dolphins danced into the air.

"Yes, Sweetie, I see! The dolphins are lovely! Thanks for showing Papa. Thank you, Jesus, for this incredible glimpse of Your creation," Aaron responded patting her leg.

As they walked slowly through the sand dunes, he could feel Angel's body slumping over and the vibrations of her head bobbing up and down. The sun shone brightly and he pulled her sleepy body from his shoulders to his arms. He adjusted her sun visor and held her close. He hummed, "Wind Beneath My Wings," as he climbed the stairs to the villa.

Maria took the exhausted princess from her dad to lay her down for a nap. Aaron could hear his daughter singing a soft lullaby. He decided to relax on the shaded veranda. Even though the wind from the ocean was invigorating, his eyes could not resist the swaying motion of the swings lull to close.

∞

The dream came swiftly as real as the rising and falling of his chest breath. Aaron could see his body sprawled on a sterilized hospital bed. Tubes extended from virtually every opening in his form. The monitor above his head displayed a straight red line and blared like a tornado siren. He lay there motionless; it was evident he was dead. As his spirit rose, he looked down upon his family surrounding his bed. Aaron could see tears streaming down Maria's, Eula's, and Brian's faces. He wanted to wrap his arms around them and tell them it would be okay, but he kept ascending through the ceiling into the brilliant night sky and upward in a millisecond, he felt light and free, no more pain. An amazing peace flooded him.

He was keenly aware of all his senses. Colors more vivid than he had ever known filled his eyes' capacities to see, jewels of green jasper, dazzling diamond, sharp crystal, fiery ruby and sparkling gold. Blinding light penetrated his soul as he approached what appeared to be the very throne of God. Clothed in pure white, hair like wool and seated on a throne of flaming fire, wheels ablaze, the Master stood and gazed upon him. Aaron fell to his knees, weeping with his arms extended in front of him. A gentle but firm hand touched his shoulder, lifted his face upwards and looked into his eyes.

"My son, you have come, welcome to your Father's house. You have been a good and faithful servant. Walk with me in the garden," Jesus voiced.

As they walked a small figure appeared playing between the lush bushes. The sparkling eyes of the child looked familiar. Aaron bent down and gazed deeply into them searching for a clue about who this youngster might be. The boy seemed enthralled with following them.

"Master, who is this lad who plays at our feet?" He inquired.

"Son, this is Isaiah. Do you remember?"

"Oh, yes! Oh, yes!" He squealed as he bent to pick up the child and twirled him in the air. The little boy laughed with glee and whispered, "Papa." Aaron's heart melted. He held him close and did not want to let him go, but Jesus looked back and beckoned him forward with His gentle eyes.

Their conversation continued.

"Not everyone who comes here has a choice to return to their earthly home, but I'm giving you that option. You can choose to stay here, or return to your family."

Aaron held tightly to the little boy. The youngster's eyes held a sparkle of freshly polished sterling. His countenance was full of contentment and joy.

"You are telling me I have the choice to stay here with you and experience no more pain, fear, suffering, or death? The chance to be with a grandson I lost but is now alive?"

"Yes, I am," He said. "However, you may decide to return home to your family and future grandchildren."

"Additional grandchildren? There will be more?" Aaron's puzzled look made Jesus smile.

"Yes. Does this surprise you? You will play a significant influence in their lives. Now walk and ponder the words I've spoken to you. Enjoy the spectacular grandeur of my creation untouched by sin as at the beginning." The Master spoke softly and then disappeared from view.

As Aaron sauntered through the fields of yellow and white daisies, his hand played lazily around the petals of the numerous flowers. He never felt such a longing to stay anywhere. He could relate to Paul in the Scriptures in a way he never truly understood until this moment, "For I am hard pressed between the two, having a desire to depart and be with Christ which is far better, nevertheless to remain in the flesh is more needful for you." (Phil. 1:23:24 NJK)

∞

Maria stood gazing at her father. The cool light breeze frolicked delicately on her sensitive skin like someone running their fingers across the nape of her neck. It brought goose bumps from her head to her toes. The sea shell wind chimes above her sounded like the tinkling of crystal.

Aaron heard distant ringing and a voice calling to him. He did not want to leave this place.

"Dad, Dad, you're crying. Are you okay?" Maria spoke sweetly.

He lazily opened his eyes not wanting to escape the scene before him.

"Yes, Honey, I'm okay. I was walking in the most splendid place. It's the same dream I've experienced repeatedly since my healing. You've heard it many times the last couple of years. You're probably tired of it by now," Aaron replied.

"No, Dad. I love it. You chose us. How could I get tired of hearing those words?" She leaned over and hugged him. "Your lunch is ready, if you would like to come in and eat. Brian and Mom will be back soon from their fishing excursion. Maybe we can talk a little before Angel wakes up. I love you, Daddy." Maria expressed

"Sounds good. Give me just a minute to bring myself back to today," he replied.

Maria opened the screen door, walked inside and shut it quietly so as not to wake Angel.

Aaron would never forget what happened after he settled in his heart to return home from Heaven's realm. All he had to do was think it and something in that moment latched hold of him like a nursing child to its mom. Strength from deep within surged through his body and sat him upright on the hospital bed. His lungs filled with breath. His heart beat again. At that moment the process of healing began. He stayed true to what Oasis of Hope Hospital taught him about nurturing spirit, soul and body. He went back for six month boosters of the Alivett treatment, took immunity enhancers and slowly gained his strength back. Now he was traveling, sharing his testimony and representing Oasis all over the country, while Larry, Brian's best friend, partnered with him in his remodeling and landscaping business. As he sat on the porch swing, all the emotions of thankfulness flooded his soul once again, and he looked toward the skies signing thank you.

As Aaron walked through the front door, he inhaled deeply, "This smells and looks delicious. Thank you!"

They had some light conversation and enjoyed their salmon salad sandwiches. It wasn't long before the little patter of feet made their way from the bedroom and climbed up into Aaron's lap at the table.

Maria started to tell her to let her Papa eat, but he raised his hand to quiet his daughter before she could speak. Angel snuggled her body into his chest and rubbed her still sleepy eyes.

"Water, Papa, water!" She demanded.

"Angel, is that how we ask Papa?" Maria corrected.

The little girl shook her head no. She cupped her fingers in the form of a C and brought it to her mouth, the sign language symbol for drink that Maria taught her. Then Angel said, "Please."

"Good job, Little Princess," Aaron replied and hugged her.

Maria held out her hand, and she slid off of Papa's lap to the floor. They walked to the refrigerator, and opened the door together. Angel delightfully pulled her cup from the shelf, along with her half-eaten almond butter and homemade strawberry jam sandwich.

She ate a few bites and laid it on the table. "Mommy, lay down with me, please?" She tugged at Maria's pant leg.

"Okay, honey." Maria winked at her dad. "Be back in a minute."

She rested next to Angel on the bed and softly stroked her curly locks. The child snuggled against her and went back to sleep. Maria scooted easily off the bed and eased out the door.

"I knew she wasn't finished napping." Maria told her dad. She took a bite of Angel's sandwich. "Mom's grown good at making old favorites with no refined sugars. This jam is delicious."

"Yeah, you should try her plum jelly. We've made a conscious effort at eating as healthy as possible since my life and death experience. We've seen the effects of dead food in accelerating cancer cells and how live food starves them. I'm glad you and your family have begun to implement some of these things into your diet as well. Brian's research is exciting. I'm thankful I could be a part of him connecting with Dr. Contreras at Oasis of Hope."

"Brian's data from the statistics at Oasis of Hope led to the beginning of his research on alternative methods of treatment for cancer patients. He's published papers in the *International Medical*

Journal, Experimental Medicine and *Nature's Medicine*. His articles received national recognition. He's fast becoming one of the leading doctors in his field choosing to use health-altering techniques. His most recent grant will send him to several countries in the next few years to gather data on new processes for treating cancer and other terminal illnesses, as well as chronic diseases. I'm very proud of him."

"Do you ever think about adopting more children?" Aaron asked.

"Brian and I've talked about it. The picture in Angel's room reminds us frequently. Timing is everything. Life has been ridiculously busy with our move to Flagstaff, Brian's job change and travel, plus planning Larry and Adaline's wedding. I've been teaching Angel her numbers, A.B.C.'s, shapes and colors. I want her ready to start pre-school next year. She is a precocious little girl, curious about everything." Maria replied

"I know, you've barely time to breathe. That's why I wanted this vacation together. I want us to remember in the busyness of life the things that are most important. I hope you and Brian will go on a date and have some time together while we're here. We'll watch Angel."

"Thanks, Dad." Maria responded.

"Did I hear someone say date?" Brian exclaimed as he bounded in the house holding a cooler. His grinning face said it all. The smell exuberating from his body left no question as to who had caught fish.

"Good catch?" Maria asked.

"Oh yes!" Eula said as she slipped past Brian.

"You stink," Maria held her nose and hand up toward Brian.

He sat the cooler down and chased Maria around the kitchen trying to hug her.

"Get away from me, you fishy freak." She slapped at him with the towel in her hand. "You're going to wake Angel up. Dad help!"

"Oh no, I'm staying out of this. Never come between a man and his wife." Aaron smiled and pulled Eula onto his lap. "How come you don't stink?" he asked.

"Because I didn't let the fish touch my clothes. I let the fishing guides bate my hook and take the fish off. I landed the biggest grouper," Eula bragged.

Brian cornered Maria, but softly leaned over and kissed her head. "Okay, you win. I'll go shower. Yes, Mom did win on the biggest fish; however, I had the largest catch of fish on the ship, twenty-two to be exact," he said as he strutted off like a peacock.

"I love the ocean. Thanks for the deep-sea fishing package. It was a great birthday gift. The dolphins followed our boat for at least thirty minutes. Their silky, shimmery skin reflecting on the waters was magical." She kissed Aaron and looked deep into his eyes. "I love you and am so grateful you are here with us." Eula caressed his face in her hands.

Maria walked out of the room to go check on Angel and give her parents some space.

Angel still slept soundly. Maria shut the door quietly and tapped on the bathroom frame. Knowing it was his wife; Brian hollered from the shower, "It's unlocked. Want to join me?" he laughed.

Maria peeked her head around the shower curtain, "No, are you hungry? Want to go for a stroll with me?"

"Well, sure, but I might get arrested if I go like this?" He mocked.

"Ha! Ha! Ha! Aren't you a funny guy?" Maria quipped.

"Yes, I'm starving, but if you make me a sandwich to take with me, I would love to stroll with you." He jumped out of the shower and grabbed her. She slapped him hard on his behind.

"Great! I'll ask Mom to keep an eye on Angel. Dad suggested we go for a date too."

From the bedroom Maria heard Angel crying, "Mommy. Mommy."

She rushed into the room, but the toddler was still sleeping. Her hair was damp with perspiration. Maria opened the window a little to allow the cool breeze to blow in. She felt her head, but she didn't appear to have a fever.

Brian popped his head in, "Is she okay?" he said quietly.

"Yeah, maybe she had a dream." Maria replied.

They walked out into the living room where Aaron and Eula were sitting comfortably.

"Do you mind if we start our date now?" Brian asked as he pulled Maria close to him.

"Go ahead. We are good." Aaron responded.

"Mom, are you sure you aren't too tired?" Maria asked.

"I'm fine sweetie. Do you mind if we take Angel to the Aquarium when she wakes up?" Eula requested.

"She will be ecstatic! Please, make sure she eats though. Lately, she's been a very picky eater. She loves green beans cooked in a little olive oil and garlic. The rest of her sandwich is in the refrigerator, and there are veggie straws in her bag with the boxed almond milks. Everything else you need is in her backpack. Thank you." Maria hugged both her parents.

"Take your time and don't worry. Now go before she wakes up," Aaron demanded.

"Mom, don't let her sleep more than an hour, or she will be grumpy," Maria said as Brian yanked her out the door. "She'll be fine, let's go play," he teased.

Chapter Two
Romantic Night

Brian and Maria sat on the deck of the seafood restaurant overlooking the tranquil ocean. The candle on the table flickered in its glass dome. The waiter placed a skillet of sizzling scallops, sautéed broccoli, mushrooms and onions, along with steaks and salmon kabobs with rice pilaf in front of them.

"Ma'am, I will be back with the rest of your order. Anything else I may get you?"

"Yes, we'll both have a glass of Sangria, and I'll take some hot sauce, please." Brian responded.

Maria gazed out over the rippling water's edge, contemplating whether to bring up the topic of adoption during this peaceful moment. She shivered.

"What are you thinking of my love? Are you cold?" Brian asked.

He stood, took off his windbreaker, settled it over her shoulders, and wrapped his arms around her.

"Better?" he questioned as he leaned over to kiss her before seating himself.

"Yes, thank you. Not really thinking about much," she said with a smile.

After the waiter brought their hot cheesy biscuits and remaining items, they prayed and ate.

"I'll let that answer go for now, but I know you too well, and you are pondering something. I can see deliberation in those beautiful blue eyes. You know you want to tell me. Besides, you have the look." He laughed.

She almost gagged on her mouthful of food and blurted out, "What look? Your imagination is getting the best of you."

"You know, the wrinkled forehead, eyes squinted, peaking over at me trying not to smile, but to be serious. Reading me, definitely reading me."

"Ah, I see. You have me pegged. You're not only a doctor, you've also become a psychologist now."

He raised his glass, "A toast to us, time together and new adventures."

She did likewise. "New adventures?"

"I have a feeling those thoughts rolling around in your head are going to bring us new escapades for sure." He snickered and leaned over the table to kiss her longingly.

She passionately responded, almost forgetting where they were in the silence of the night and the crashing waves against the rocks.

Chapter Three
HEATED CONFRONTATION

Larry and Adaline drove down the long winding cobblestone drive, past the roman goddess fountain and flower gardens. She tremored. The meeting with her parents, Frederick and Beatrice, brought back horrifying memories of the night Larry was introduced to them. Her heart broke at her father's refusal to give her away to "a man of low means, not good enough."

The conversation played over in Adaline's mind like an old song repeating itself. This trip was Larry's idea, and he felt compelled to try to convince them of reconciliation for everyone's sake. They decided not to tell them of the pregnancy for now. He only wanted to give them the opportunity to be part of the wedding and their lives.

Larry pressed the door bell, and it resounded its mournful, loud tone, like one from the old *The Munsters'* series. Adaline fidgeted on the entryway step. It seemed like an eternity before anyone answered. The maid would be off tonight leaving one of her parents to answer their call.

"Good evening. Do come in." Frederick said with a tone as flat as his tall frame.

"Thank you." Larry said as he took Adaline's quaking hand.

They followed him into the immense, plush sitting area. The maroon rug delicately flowered with white petals and chrysotile patterns complemented the contemporary America Waylee furniture.

"Your mother isn't feeling well. She may join us later if her migraine dissipates," Adaline's father commented. "Would you like some brandy?"

"No, thank you." Larry answered for them both.

"My dear, has the cat stolen your tongue? The last time I saw you, you had no problem answering for yourself." He looked wryly at Larry.

"No, father," Adaline said.

"Let's get down to business, shall we? Our position has not changed. We expect our daughter to marry someone of her standard and upbringing. I've looked into your background, and you do not qualify." He said smugly, looking in Larry's direction.

"Sir, with all due respect, my family's background does not dictate who I am. I love your daughter. I have a good job. I will soon be a partner in the landscaping business I currently work for. I'll take good care of her. We want you and her mother to be a part of our lives. The restoration of this relationship is important to us," Larry responded, holding back his temper.

"Father, please, we'll be getting married soon, and we want you to be there. It would not be the same without my parents. We've been distant the last few months because your rejection hurt us deeply, but we've forgiven and moved on. We hope you'll find it in your heart to accept our marriage relationship," Adaline implored.

Beatrice sauntered down the spiral staircase. Her exquisite A-line ¾ sleeves appliqué court train evening gown made her look more like someone going to a ball, rather than someone with a migraine dressed for bed. "Dear, pour me a drink. I'm sure this conversation will only excruciate my pain further."

She leaned over and kissed Adaline lightly on the cheek. "You looked flushed. Why do you insist on bringing this man to our home? We relayed our feelings to you the last time we spoke. Your whining and his appearance won't change our minds. It's obvious you don't belong together. You look miserable," Beatrice remarked.

Adaline stood up, "How dare you! I would think you would be excited I've found a man who loves me and wants to take care of me. You'll never change. Money is all you see. I don't know why I expected differently. Actually, I didn't. He did." She pointed to Larry. "Nana is the only one who ever understood me. You never tried to. I feel sorry for you. One day you will grow old and be all alone. There are things your money can't buy. I've found the true source of love, happiness, and peace. I'll live for Jesus with abandon and love the man He chose for me."

"Well, there are two men in your life we'll never accept. Jesus is for fantasy and weaklings," Frederick responded.

She turned to Larry. "Let's go!"

Larry looked on them with pity. "I hope one day you will change your minds."

They walked out the front door and did not look back. Her parents closed the door behind them. "Can you believe the audacity of that child?" Beatrice said as she poured herself another drink.

Adaline and Larry got in the car. They remained silent on the drive to her apartment. He walked her to the door. "I'm sorry I let you down. You were right. I thought we could change their minds, but obviously they are stuck in their ways. Do you want me to come in and stay with you a little while?" he asked sympathetically.

"You didn't let me down. I need some time alone. Are we leaving early in the morning? I need to stop by Michaels at some point. Maybe on the way we can take a break and do a little shopping."

"I want to be on the road by 6 am if you're feeling up to it." He kissed her, and she clung tightly to him.

"I've never felt as accepted as I do when I'm in your arms. I love you," Adaline expressed.

"I love you too." He opened the door for her, and she slipped inside.

∞

Morning came way too early for Adaline. The night's episode with her parents left her exhausted. Larry called and woke her up as promised. She felt nauseated. The doctor said she could take the motion sickness tablets moderately. Her instinct led her to take them since they would be in the car most of the day.

Larry knocked on her door promptly at 7 am. He helped her load her suitcase in his truck.

He looked at her rosy cheeks and said, "You okay?"

She shook her head yes.

"Do you think they'll be angry with us? Maria worked hard at planning the wedding for us. This seems impulsive and so unlike me. I'm nervous." Adaline stated, trying to work through her ever-changing emotions.

"Honey, it'll be okay. The beach is a great place to say our vows. We prayed about this and felt at peace. We messed up, but we've asked Jesus' forgiveness, and now we just need to make it right. I love you. I've shown my commitment to you by completing the *Courageous* study and signing the contract. This course has taught me what God expects out of me as a husband and father. Now, we're going to make it legal. We have our marriage certificate with us. Pastor Stroke and Aaron can do the ceremony. Angel can still be our flower girl. Maria and Brian can stand with us. It's simple, just like we wanted. We'll treasure it always. Then we can bring our baby into the world as a family," Larry replied compassionately.

Adaline started weeping, "I love you! I'm thankful Jesus forgives us. I know our friends will stand beside us. I pray Maria won't be too disappointed. I'm sorry my parents won't be here, but it is their choice, not ours. It saddens me, though."

"I know honey. Let's focus on the good, walk through our emotions as they come and maybe one day your parents will understand. When they see how much I love you and take care of you, they won't be able to resist loving me."

"Right. Aaron knows we're coming? You did ask him?"

Larry smiled sheepishly, but didn't answer.

"Larry Edward! You did talk to Aaron?" she persisted as she poked him in the ribs.

He jumped, "Hey, I'm driving. Of course, silly, he said yes, and he wouldn't spoil our surprise. Now relax and enjoy the ride."

Adaline adjusted her car pillow behind her head and turned the radio to 90.3, the local KFLR station. She needed the uplifting music to calm her frazzled soul. The song, "Good, Good Father" by Chris Tomlin rang out over the speakers. Larry smiled and rubbed her arm as she drifted off to sleep.

Chapter Four
STORMY NIGHT

Brian and Maria finished their meal and walked hand-in-hand along the peer high above the crashing waves. Clouds began to roll in. They could see lightening careening through the dark sky in the distance. It displayed its spectacular power to the tune of Mozart.

"Maybe we should get back!" Maria yelled above the storm's coming rage.

"Oh no, you haven't told me what you were thinking yet." Brian said as he slightly tightened his arms around her and snuggled his head into the nap of her neck, kissing her ever so fervidly.

"You've got to be kidding! This storm is coming in fast, and you are making me cold!" She tried to whirl around to face him, but he refused to let her go.

Playfully he said, "Not before I kiss the other side. You've always said if I kiss one side I've got to kiss the other."

"Oh, my goodness," She giggled, "That's only when I'm doing dishes and you sneak up behind me."

He loosened his grip and she slid around to face him as her back leaned against the railing.

"Are you trying to get me excited?"

"Ha! Ha! You are easily excitable. Maybe I am. She broke free from his hold and started to run. "If you catch me, I'll tell you!" she yelled breathlessly.

"That's easy enough." Brain hollered just as he tripped and toppled to the ground. "Ouch, Ohhh, Oh Man!"

"Brian are you okay?" Maria sprinted back to his side.

Holding his ankle he grimaced. "My sandal caught in the plank?" "You'll do anything to win! Let me see!" she demanded as she pried his finger away to take a look.

He started laughing gleefully and pulled her down into his arms. "You snake; you cheated!"

"Yeah, but I got my prize, didn't I? Now tell me what's going on?"

"Dad asked me today if we were going to adopt more children. I told him I didn't know. Life's been busy, and we hadn't time to think about it." Maria let a tear trickle down her face.

Brian wiped it away. "You said you didn't want to think about adopting until Angel grew older, so I let it go. I had no idea you felt this way."

"I did, but I've been thinking of it more since the investigators told us there was no evidence of the man who shot Uncle Ron and the look-alike who appeared at our door the same day. Before I was scared. Since everything happened to Dad, I've realized life's too short to live in fear. It wastes precious time and energy. I even let Angel sleep with the window opened a little today. Rojomen did say he had our backs, even if we couldn't see him watching over us."

"You know this year is one of my busiest travel years, but the adoption process usually takes at least a year or more. I want us to fulfill the dream God gave us after we lost Isaiah. The picture on the nursery wall reminds me every day of the vision. You know I believe it to be a gift from God. Why don't we start by contacting the agency we used before? Maybe we can get an infant boy from another country with the same ethnicity of Angel?"

"Sounds wonderful, but how do we know where to request a child from? We really don't know her original background," she said as she clung to him, "Dad will be ecstatic."

"We'll figure it out. Now help me up, please. I feel rain droplets on my arm. I really did twist my angle, but it's okay. I'll ice it when we get back."

The rain started to come in torrents as they ran back to the car.

"I'll drive." Maria shouted.

"No, I got this! Rain's too heavy," he said as he opened her door.

"Always a gentleman first, I love it! Our son will learn to be a good man."

They both were soaked to the bone. Maria pulled towels from behind her seat and dabbed his face. "You know those eyes always mesmerize me." The thunder roared and startled her as she leaned over to kiss Brian. With a worried look she said, "I hope Mom and Dad made it back before this storm hit."

"I'm sure they're fine. Your dad is good about checking the storm radar. They may have decided to stay in."

Maria pulled her phone from the glove compartment and dialed her mom's number. "Yeah, but these ocean blasts move in pretty fast. No answer!"

"Now hon, calm down, breathe. It's going to be okay. Don't let your mind go racing. Mindfulness, remember? I'm sure they're at the house." Even as Brian tried to soothe Maria's fears, his own were trying to overtake his heart.

The rain fell heavy and Brian could barely see the road. He eased his way through the winding path back to the bungalow. Maria prayed the whole way back. No cars were in the driveway as they pulled up to the back door. Her face went flush.

"Honey, go in, and I'll pull up further so they can get closer to the door when they come home."

Maria fumbled with her keys and finally got the entryway open. She looked around and noticed her dad's phone plugged into the charger.

"Great!" she said as Brian walked in. "Dad left his phone."

"Honey, you're shivering. Go change, and I'll try your mom's phone again."

Eula's phone rang and rang, but no answer.

∞

Aaron and Eula decided to pull into a local restaurant to let the storm die down or pass. She rocked Angel back and forth to calm her. The deep rumbling of thunder and jagged streaks of lightning frightened the child. She wrapped her arms around her grandma's shoulders, buried her head in Eula's chest, and held on for dear life.

Aaron sat sipping on his coffee. "Hon, is your phone ringing?"

"Oh yes, can you grab it?"

He answered the phone and calmed Brian's frantic voice on the other end, reassuring him they were fine and would start back when the rain lightened.

Maria and Brian were relieved.

"Okay, now that dilemma is solved. Where were we?" Brian expressed as he sauntered over to his wife who lay under a fleece blanket on the coach.

∞

Larry peered over at his now sleeping beauty. His heart exploded with thankfulness for this woman God united his heart with and the baby in her womb. He prayed he would be a good father. He hadn't anticipated such bad weather; it was getting dark, and they had been driving in the rain a few hours. The clock on the dash shone 6:30 pm.

Larry nudged Adaline, "Honey, do you want to stop and eat, or keep driving?"

"How far do we have to go? It's still raining. Arrrgh! I've gotta pee!"

"I would say about two or so hours. Look, there's a diner. I can pull right up to the door and let you out."

"Yes, please. Thanks." Adaline expressed. She hurried out of the car and spotted the restroom sign. "I'd no idea pregnancy could make you use the bathroom this much," she whispered.

A lady in the next stall piped up, "Oh sweetie, you have no idea. Wait until you're in the third trimester."

"You didn't see me come in, how do you know how far along I am." Adaline asked.

"I saw through the crack in the door," the woman laughed. "You are in for a few surprises."

Adaline felt a little perturbed as this lady's assumption she was inexperienced and knew nothing about her pregnancy. The feeling quickly passed as the lady's kind, warm voice continued.

"I bore eight children and raised nine. Each pregnancy differed; none were exactly the same, just like my kids. They each are unique and special, God's jewels and gifts to me."

The lady left her bathroom stall and began washing her hands. Adaline soon followed. She smiled at the plump woman with soft white hair and penetrating hazel eyes. They held a glow and wisdom behind them.

A feeling of sincere humility swept over Adaline, and she asked, "I'm a new mom. Do you have any advice for me? I'm not close to my parents, and it saddens me I can't turn to my mother."

"I'm sorry honey." The kind woman responded. "The best advice I can give you is to cherish every moment and trust God to lead you every day. May I give you a hug?"

"Yes, please." Adaline couldn't stop the trickling tears, although she tried to choke them back. "I'm sorry, so emotional these days."

The sweet lady hugged her genuinely and firm. She placed a piece of paper in Adaline's hand. "If you ever need a prayer or to talk, call me. I often counsel people over the telephone. It's my ministry. Remember, our meeting wasn't by chance. God loves you very much.

He planned for us to be here today. Don't ever forget, He loves you, sweet child."

"Thank you, thank you. I needed to hear your words. I've made many mistakes."

"I know, but this baby is no accident. Jesus has a purpose for his little life."

The lady turned to walk away, and as she put her hand on the door knob.

Adaline pleaded, "Wait, how do you know it's a he?"

She smiled brightly, "Pray about the name, Joshua, it means, "Jehovah is generous." In the Bible Joshua conquered mountains and believed when no one else did. Gotta go now. My daughter will be in here after me, thinking something is wrong." She hugged her one last time.

Adaline washed her face and marveled at what happened. Someone knocked on the door.

Larry hollered in, "Honey, are you okay?"

"Yes, I'd the most amazing experience ever!" She looked around for the woman, but she was nowhere to be found. If it wasn't for the piece of paper with the phone number on it, she would have thought she was dreaming.

"You okay? I've a table for us over here." Larry guided her.

"Yes, I'm famished, but I need to tell you what happened. It was Divine." Adaline relayed the whole story to Larry, making sure not to leave out any details. The more she talked, the wider his smile became until it engulfed his entire face.

Thrilled at the declaration of them having a boy, Larry shouted, "I like Joshua. He conquered mountains! Whoopee! A boy! God's giving me a son."

∞

Aaron, Eula and Angel arrived at the cottage around midnight. They texted to let Brian and Maria know they were on the way. The two fell asleep holding each other on the coach. As the key jiggled in the door, it startled Brian and he jumped up, knocking Maria to the floor.

"Oh Babe, I'm sorry." He said sympathetically.

He held his hand out to help her up. She could hear the gentle patter of rain against the roof.

"You made it." Maria expressed, taking her daughter from her mother's arms.

Angel rubbed her sleepy eyes. "Mommy," she screeched.

"Some of the roads were washed out due to the heavy rain, so we kept getting re-routed." Aaron sighed deeply.

"You look exhausted. Thanks for taking her," Brian responded.

Eula hugged them both. "I'm just glad everyone is safe. Thank God! I'm too wound up for bed. Coffee anyone?"

"Sure, since we are going to stay up anyway, do you want to tell them our good news?" Brian asked.

Maria looked at Brian. He cocked his eyebrow, "Well, are you going to, or should I?"

"Go ahead honey," she said.

Everyone sat down at the kitchen table.

Angel pulled at Brian's sleeve, "What's the news, Daddy? Are we getting a puppy?"

He boosted her up on his lap, "How would you like mommy and daddy to get you a little brother or sister?"

The child giggled with glee and clapped her hands. "Yes, yes, my very own baby."

All the adults laughed.

"We are happy you've decided to adopt another child." Aaron said.

"What does a-dupt mean?" Angel asked.

Brian gently turned her face to him. "It means we go pick a child, or a child picks us."

The three year old kept asking questions until Maria said, "Okay, it's time we put you to bed. Mommy will explain more another day." This wasn't a question she anticipated answering, and she wasn't prepared. She eyed her dad gingerly.

No sooner had she gotten Angel to sleep and was about to head that direction herself, when she heard the crackling of tires on the gravel coming up the drive.

"My goodness, who could that be at this late hour?" Brian questioned.

Maria peered out the window shade, "It looks like Larry's truck."

"Oh, amongst all the commotion, I forgot to tell you they were coming. I invited them some time ago, and they said no, but they phoned this morning and asked if it would be okay if they joined us after all." Aaron shrugged his shoulders. "We've the spare room." He chimed in.

As they stood on the porch, Larry held the umbrella for Adaline, tapped on the door and assured her everything would be okay.

Brian slung the door open, nearly knocking Larry to the ground. "Welcome to the party, late as usual." He gave them a bear hug.

"Okay, let them in. Shhh. Angel is asleep. What on earth are you doing driving in this weather?" Maria asked.

Aaron took the umbrella and Adaline's bag.

"Well, when I checked the forecast this morning, it said, "cloudy with a chance of isolated showers," Larry replied.

"Yes, it did!" Aaron piped up.

"We are pleased you came. You are family too. Coffee?" Eula asked.

"We were telling mom and dad we are filing papers to adopt again." Brian said.

"That's wonderful." Adaline hugged Maria.

"Congratulations! We've our own news." Larry said as he wrapped his arm around Adaline's shoulder.

Her face went white, and she looked as if she would faint.

Brian took notice and helped Larry escort her to the coach to sit down. "Maria, will you get a glass of water and cold cloth please?" He started taking her pulse. "Are you okay?" he asked.

"Yes, all the excitement, I guess." Adaline responded weakly.

Maria dabbed her forehead and placed the cold compress on her neck.

"Sweetie, I'm sorry. Do you want to wait until tomorrow? I should've asked you first." Larry questioned.

"No, it's okay. Go ahead." Adaline said.

Larry clasped her hand. "Pastor Stroke and Aaron are going to marry us on the beach as soon as this weather clears up."

Maria's face flushed a bright red. She retreated hastily to the bathroom. "How could they do this, after all the planning and work I've done?" The voice of frustration echoed off the walls back at her. She stewed in her anger for several moments before hearing Adaline crying softly in the living room. Her selfish heart melted.

The men had retreated outside and talked quietly on the veranda. The screen door let the cool night breeze blow in. Maria walked over and shut the back egress, giving her mind time to process the words ready to come forth from her lips.

She went into the living room and sat close to Adaline. "Why change the wedding plans? We've worked so hard to make it what you wanted?" Maria blurted.

"I know. We're sorry for that, but..." Adaline lowered her head and choked back the lump in her throat.

The men came inside. Larry responded for her, "We decided to move up the wedding date because something more pressing has come up."

"More pressing than your own wedding?" Maria glared at him.

"Yes," Adaline said softly and rubbed her abdomen.

Eula came in from cleaning up the kitchen.

Maria gasped, embarrassed at her own insensitivity. Brian came over and pulled her over to sit beside him, gently taking hold of her hand.

"I thought you were going to wait." Maria sighed.

"Let them explain." Brian reprimanded.

"We were, but we didn't. It wasn't planned. We got carried away. We want to make things right." Larry reasoned.

Aaron grabbed Eula's hand and stood beside Larry. They held hands and made a circle around Adaline. "We're your family, and we'll stand beside you in this journey." Aaron prayed and then asked everyone to go to bed. They would finish the conversation later in the morning. Eula showed Larry and Adaline to their room.

"This is lovely. Thank you for everything. You've both been like parents to us." Adaline hugged Eula.

"Oh sweetie, I'm thankful we can be. Sleep well." She eyed Larry.

"We'll behave. I promise." Larry responded.

"If he doesn't, he'll sleep on the coach tomorrow night," Eula demanded.

Adaline giggled.

"Very well, good night." She softly closed their door.

Chapter Five
RISING ABOVE

Maria tossed and turned until she couldn't take it anymore. She slipped out from underneath Brian's arm and pulled the cover up over Angel who was sleeping on the cot at the end of their bed, and then tip toed quietly out of the room. She made a cup of chamomile tea, grabbed her Bible, and sat in the recliner, but try as she might she could not focus.

"Lord, I confess I'm angry, stewing actually. They promised to remain pure, and I've put a lot of work, money, and time into planning this wedding. Good thing we haven't mailed out the invitations yet. I'll have to cancel everything. How selfish can Larry be? Okay, I know, it takes two, but this is not the way to start their marriage. Arrgh!" She grumbled and slammed her cup down, spilling tea. "Oh no, that's great, just great!" She moved her Bible and ran for paper towels. In the process of cleaning up her mess, she remembered the saying she strived to teach Angel, "When we do something we shouldn't, messes always happen, so it's better to do the right thing the first time. Right = Might." She stopped and paused.

Maria heard the still small voice of the Lord, "I work all things together for good to those who love me, My Child. Trust me. Forgive and show my love. Then you will have my peace, and all will be well with your soul."

She knelt by the chair, "Daddy, I'm sorry. I do forgive and know this won't be the first time I've a bad attitude during this process, so I ask for Your guidance. You are my very present help in time of need. Thank you." In the past when Maria needed to show mercy and struggled with it, she would watch the movie, *The Nativity*, so she popped it in the DVD player and lowered the volume.

Brian woke up and felt the bed next to him. Angel had climbed up beside him at some point in the night, but Maria wasn't there. He knew she felt cheated by the news and their guests' arrival. They looked forward to this alone time with her parents. He snuggled the covers around Angel and slipped his pillow next to her back as he crept out of bed. His sneaky maneuvers did not work. As he opened the door it creaked, and Angel started to whimper.

"Daddy, Daddy."

"Okay, honey. Daddy's here." He took her in his arms and cradled her close. "Let's go find Mommy."

Angel nodded her sleepy head. Brian looked around the semi-light living room, trying to adjust his eyes, but Angel spotted her first and pointed, "There's Mommy." She wiggled down out of Brian's arms, and before he could grab her, she climbed onto Maria's sprawled out body. "Mommy. Mommy, I'm hungry." She sat on Maria's stomach and tugged on the cover to pull it from her face. "Wake up, wake up." The little girl squealed.

Maria sat up quickly and started tickling Angel. The child cackled with amusement.

"Arrr Maties', did someone say breakfast?" Aaron replied as he came around the corner. "How about pirate pancakes?" he asked.

"Yes, Papa, can I help?" She ran and threw her arms around his legs and gathered her feet up on his toes.

"Sure enough, Princess. What's a pirate party without a princess?" Aaron replied.

"Dad, how much time do I have? Can I crash for thirty more minutes?" Maria asked.

"Me too, Brian piped up. If she's going back to bed, so am I." He tickled her feet.

"Scat you two, making this entire ruckus; you're going to wake our other sleeping guests. Hon, I'll help you." Eula mustered as she came in the room.

As Eula set the table, she looked out toward the beach and saw Adaline and Larry holding hands walking. "They aren't asleep after all. They're adorable together. He's come such a long way since Pastor Stroke mentored him and he's been working with you. You are such a good example of a loving husband!" Eula exclaimed.

Aaron didn't respond as he and Angel chatted merrily about the delicious pancakes they were fixing to gobble down.

"Now, go wake your mommy and daddy," Aaron said as he sat her down on the floor from the stool she stood on.

"No, wait. You first need to help Mema finish setting the table before you go bouncing on their heads," Eula commented.

She puckered her lip out, but conceded.

∞

"Maria seemed pretty upset last night. Do you think we are doing the right thing? She did a lot of work preparing for the wedding." Adaline questioned twisting her fingers tightly together as they stood on the boat dock.

"I do, but we'll do whatever you want to. I'd like to be married now. I love you. I want to be with you all of the time and take care of you." Larry affirmed.

"I want that too, more than anything.

Larry leaned over and kissed her. "Look, we can still have the reception. Right? We'll talk to Maria about it. I think she'll understand. Only the deposits have been paid on the bookings. It will be fine. It'll be beautiful to have our wedding on the beach, with the sun shining off the water and our toes in the sand. Very romantic. They're here for another week. The weather is cloudy today, but it's supposed to clear out tonight. Let's see what their plans are and work around their vacation. I work for Aaron, and the assignments he gave me are complete. We should be good for a few days."

"Breakfast" Eula hollered. She decided to move the silverware out on the porch table since it was such a nice morning, the humidity tempered only by the ocean breeze.

Angel bounded up on top of Maria and Brian. They were pretending to be asleep, so they seized upon the perfect opportunity to wrap her in the blanket and tickle her until she squealed.

"It's time to eat. Let me out or I'll tell Papa on you." Angel sneered.

They made their way out to the others. Everyone sat down, held hands and prayed. Adaline squeezed Maria's hand apologetically. Maria smiled at her sweet gesture.

"Dig in. No one likes cold pancakes," Aaron demanded.

"I do," cackled Angel. "I like them anyway."

"We've something to say," Larry commented.

"Not before devotional," Eula quipped.

She opened the page and began to read, "Forgive others just as Christ forgave you." The devotional went on to talk about seeing others through Jesus' eyes, helping them rise above their current condition.

"Mom, that's good. Where did you get it?" Maria asked.

"I've never seen it before. It was on the table under your Bible by the recliner. I thought it belonged to you. It says, CMA on the cover, changing one heart at a time." Eula responded.

"Pancakes are delicious, Dad. You outdid yourself this time," Brian complemented.

"Thanks. CMA is the Christian Motorcyclists Association. I talked to one of their guys at the gas station during the storm. He pulled in to wait it out. We have a lot in common, and I told him I would come share my story at their meeting some time. My dad rode a Harley soft tail for years, and when your mom and I first got married I owned a Honda Aspencade," Aaron explained.

"I don't remember a motorcycle." Maria eyed her dad.

"It was before you were born," he said as he got up and hugged her. "This is my little girl, Angel."

"Oh dad," Maria blushed.

Larry cleared his throat in another attempt to speak up, but Eula wanted to pray first. Then she started cleaning up the dishes. She turned toward him and asked, "Will you help me in the kitchen please." She twitched her head in the direction of the door.

"Yes, Ma'am," Larry said affectionately.

Aaron and Brian took the hint and started walking toward the beach, Angel in tow.

"Swing me, please. One, two, three," She counted.

The men each took a hand and to her delight, swung her high in the air every few steps.

Adaline and Maria sat quietly at the table.

"Maria, I'm really sorry. I'm sorry we've disappointed you. I'm sorry you've worked so hard, and we're ruining your plans. Please, forgive us. Your relationship means a great deal to me. Maybe we are being selfish, but we don't want to wait. We want to be together more than anything, and we want it to be right before God. Larry wants to take care of me and the baby. If you want us to help cancel arrangements we can. We thought we would keep the reception booked as is, if that's okay with you? We want your forgiveness and blessing. May we have the wedding here? The beach is gorgeous. I'm nervous and rambling," Adaline described their desires.

Between the worry and excitement Adaline started feeling queasy. "Oh no, I think I'm going to throw up." She stood to lean over the balcony.

Maria felt sorry for her and popped her head into the kitchen. "Mom, will you bring a rag and cup of ginger ale, please?" She dabbed Adaline's face as she sipped on the cold drink.

"I'm not going to lie. I'm disappointed and hurt, but I forgive you. I want you both to be happy. I don't want you to worry; it's not good for you or your baby. Have you been sick a lot? The saltines and ginger ale helped me a lot during my pregnancy."

"Not really, mainly this trip. I'm barely in my first trimester. I do notice if I get nervous, excited, or upset, I get more nauseated."

"Look, if you want to have the wedding here, I'm good with it. I want what is best for you, and if it's what you really want, I'll be okay. I bless your decision."

Adaline threw her arms around Maria's neck. "Thank you, I love you, my friend."

"Now what are we going to do about flowers?" Maria queried.

Larry stuck his head out the door and inquired, "Are you okay, Honey?"

Maria threw the damp rag and it went swirling past his head. "She's fine."

"Ya'll are like siblings. I've silk arrangements in the car. The restaurant we stopped at carried a few, not a lot, but enough for our ingenious minds to work with. I want to create a small flower ringlet for my hair and corsage for Larry's vest. We're going casual, but pretty. No shoes. We want our toes touching the sand," Adaline responded.

"You've thought this out?" Maria questioned.

"To be honest, it's what I dreamed of as a girl." Adaline smiled brightly.

Eula came out the door with a small cup in her hand, "May I join you?"

"Sure, we are talking about their wedding. Adaline knows what she wants. Sounds simplistic enough," Maria said.

"Good, we like easy around here. After all, we are on vacation." Eula reciprocated.

Adaline started to apologize, but Eula put her hand up and patted her arm. "None of that, there's been enough explanations for one day.

I wouldn't have it any other way. Let me go grab my planner." She scurried back in the house.

"Where's Larry?" Adaline asked.

"He snuck out the side door to go find the men. I guess he has his own reckoning to do. Friday looks like the best day. Will it work for you gals? I've a gorgeous sun dress and hat I brought to surprise Aaron on our date trip, but I'm afraid he only has shorts and a Hawaiian shirt. You know the blue one with big white flowers all over it? The saving grace is it matches my dress. What about you, Brian and Angel?" Eula girlishly enquired.

"Mom, slow down. You are going to make Adaline queasy again." Maria challenged.

"No, it's okay. Whatever works best for ya'll." Adaline responded.

"Let's wait until the men return. Brian and I'll want to run in town for a few things and we need to check Friday's weather. Angel needs a sundress to be a flower girl, if you are still having her do it?" Maria snapped.

"Okay, no need to get your panties in a wad. Friday is the only day our calendar is perfectly clear, "Eula retorted.

Adaline burst out laughing, "Where did you get that saying from?"

Maria could not contain herself either. They were rolling, tears streaming down their faces when the men walked up the stairs from the beach.

"What's so funny?" Brian asked.

That only made the situation worse.

"Case of the giggles, I guess?" Larry shrugged his shoulders.

"Oh, my goodness, stop you two!" Eula demanded as she jumped up and ran inside.

The laughter eased and Maria joined Brian on the swing. "Where are Angel and Dad?"

"She wasn't ready to leave yet. Papa's letting her splash her feet in the water and chase the tide back and forth," Brian answered.

Larry and Adaline stood up. "You wore her out. We are going to take a nap. Is there a coffee shop close? Maybe we can all go for a ride in a bit?" Larry commented.

"We'll check with Mom and see what's on the schedule today." Maria said.

Larry nodded and grabbed Adaline's hand. No sooner had they got inside the door when Brian heard Aaron screaming, "Brian help! Help me, please!"

Brian ran down the steps. Maria ran to get his medical kit from the car. They could see Aaron carrying Angel's unmoving body and trying to run in the sand.

Breathlessly Maria yelled for her mom – Call 911, now!"

"What happened?" Brian demanded.

"I don't know. I think a sting ray got her. She was playing at the edge of the water, screamed, and fell. I caught her, but she's not responding to me. Oh God, help us!" Aaron pleaded.

Brian took the child and laid her flat on the ground. "She's not breathing." He said as he began CPR.

Aaron knelt on the ground and sobbed. Maria ran to Brian's side. Her mom not far behind gathered her husband in her arms and prayed.

"Maria, take over!" Brain switched places with Maria and searched frantically in his bag. He gave his child a shot of adrenaline to get the heart to respond. Within seconds, Angel coughed and threw up. Brian rolled her to her side and cleared her throat and nose. "Her heartbeat is slow and respiration shallow, but she's breathing."

"There they are!" Larry hollered and pointed the EMT's in their direction.

The paramedics took over as Brian filled them in. He told them he was a doctor and the child's father.

"Honey, ride with them please," Maria pleaded with Brian as she squeezed his hand.

Adaline wrapped her arms around Maria, who almost collapsed.

"We'll bring everyone else right behind you," Larry comforted.

The fireman gave the family directions to the nearest hospital.

"Maria, I'm so sorry. I shouldn't have let her play that close to the water. She was having so much fun, and it's warmer today. I thought she'd be okay," Aaron apologized.

"Dad, it's not your fault." Maria consoled.

"We can all fit in my truck." Larry said as he herded them toward his vehicle.

No one argued. They all piled in.

In shock Aaron asked, "Why would a sting ray be this close to the beach area? I don't understand."

Eula tried to comfort him, but she trembled herself. "It's amazing how a day can go from sunlight to darkness so quickly. She'll be okay, Sweetie, tough as nails that little one. Like her Papa."

In the ambulance the EMT started an IV. Angel lay limp on the gurney. Brian stroked her hair. "It's going to be okay, Princess. Daddy is here. I'm sorry I wasn't there to protect you from mean old stingray."

The EMT slung the doors open to the ambulance, lowered the gurney and rushed in the emergency entrance.

Brian grabbed a paramedic's arm, "Is she going to be okay? Be honest with me?"

"I've never seen a child this small get stung before, but you acted quickly, and it may save her life. I pray so." The EMT put his hand on Brian's shoulder and gave a compassionate squeeze.

The rest of the family came barreling through the door.

"Where is she?" Maria fell into Brian's arms.

"Is she going to be okay?" Aaron questioned.

"The bathroom, please?" Adaline shook. Larry took her arm and pointed her to the sign.

'I'll go with her." Eula said.

I don't know yet. The doctor asked me to wait here until they could examine her. She is breathing shallowly, but her pulse seemed slightly better. Brian responded.

They clung to each other and prayed.

A nurse walked over and smiled. "There is a little girl in there asking for her mommy. Would that happen to be you?"

Brian motioned for Maria to go, and he called Pastor Stroke to get Angel on the prayer chain. He knew danger lurked in hidden places with this kind of injury. He wanted to stomp on the evil monster before anything could happen.

The hospital bed swallowed Angel's petite frame. Her foot wrapped in ice barely allowed Maria to see the discoloration and swelling along the edges of the dorsal.

"Mommy, Mommy!" Angel cried.

"Here, I am Sweetie." Maria sat on the bed and cradled the child, trying not to interfere with the oxygen tube running to her nose and the IV in her arm.

"Mommy, where's Papa? Tell him not to cry."

"Oh, you don't worry now. Papa's okay." Maria turned to the nurse as she assured Angel. "May the rest of my family come in now or at least her Daddy?" she asked.

"As you can see the room is small. The doctor will be in soon. When he returns, he wants to consult with you and your husband. For now he's asked for only one family member at a time." The nurse replied.

"Mommy, my foot hurts real bad!" Angel screamed.

Maria laid her hand as close to Angel's wound as she could without touching it or disturbing the bandage, and prayed.

"I've given her some pain medication, but the doctor doesn't want her sedated too heavily yet."

The doctor walked in, "Mrs. Frigmann, will you and your husband meet me in the conference room two doors down?"

"Yes, certainly. Mommy will be right back. Mema will come in, okay?" Maria kissed Angel on her forehead. Maria stepped out and motioned for Brian and her mom.

"Mom, please go in with her. Oh, you have her stuffed doggie. Very good. Dad, you can't go in yet, but soon. She is asking for you and told you not to cry. Brian, the doctor wants to see us."

"Mr. and Mrs. Frigmann, this is serious. Adults have died from a stingray's injection. Luckily you reacted quickly and got her responsive, which is crucial; however, her heart rate keeps dropping and the swelling in her foot is concerning. We need to place a slit in the wound to release some pressure, try to get the swelling to come down and the circulation flowing to it, or she will lose it. There are risks involved: infection, the venom traveling through the blood stream to other organs, and her heart could literally stop again. The antidote for the sting is being flown in as we speak, but it could take a few hours. There is a possibility if her heart rate drops too low, we'll lose her. We'll do everything we can to save her and the foot. It appears she is quiet the fighter. I'm hopeful with the procedure and antidote, she will pull through this and make a full recovery. Do I have your permission to do the procedure?" he asked.

"Yes, do you believe in the power of prayer? We do. Our little girl is a fighter, and she's going to make it with her foot intact. We've come too far to lose her now." Brian answered.

"I do. Now excuse me, please." He started to leave and turned back around, "One more thing, I won't be able to put her under to do the procedure. I can numb the area. I may need you to help hold her down." The doctor answered.

Tears streamed down Maria's face, "I don't know if I can do this."

"Let me ask your dad." Brian comforted her.

He explained in layman terms to Aaron, Larry and Adaline without scaring them what the doctor communicated to them. He asked Aaron if he would be strong enough to help hold Angel down under the pressure. Aaron agreed. Maria and Eula held hands in the waiting room. They all silently prayed.

Aaron looked down into those big, dark eyes with huge tears cascading like a waterfall. The nurse tied her small arms to the bed railing. Brian lay across her small torso pinning her legs down. She screamed in agony and terror as the doctor sliced into the wound releasing blood and thick yellow fluid.

"That's good, the venom is seeping out. You're doing real good, Angel. We are almost done sweetie. Hold still now. Your daddy and papa are only doing what I told them too. Good girl." The doctor cleaned up the surrounding area and inserted a tube to drain the discharge.

The nurse dabbed Angel's perspiring brow. "You are a tough little girl."

"I'm strong," Angel whimpered.

Aaron and Brian moved to the sides of the bed.

"Papa loves you to the stars." Tears filled his eyes.

She raised her now free arms up the best she could to pull his face to hers and pressed her tiny lips to his cheek. "It's okay, Papa. I'm thirsty. Water please?"

The doctor told the nurse to give her small sips of water and watch her closely.

"I don't want to move her yet. It's still too dangerous. She needs to remain still. If she remains stable after the antidote, we will move her to Pediatrics ICU for twenty-four hour observation. Keep those prayers coming," he told Brian.

"You bet! Never stop."

The nurse allowed each family member to see Angel one at a time for a few minutes.

Brian told Larry, "Take Adaline back to the house to rest along with Mom, please."

He persuaded them that they would need the car seat when Angel was released. Eula refused to leave. She could be as stubborn as Brian. She agreed to go retrieve coffee from the cafeteria, so Aaron went to help her.

"You look worried. Honey, she's going to be okay. Eula comforted Aaron.

"I feel sorry for the poor little thing. I don't want her to be scared of the ocean."

"Kids bounce back. She's ferocious and bold. I think she'll bite it back." Eula smiled

Aaron sat the coffee on the table and pulled her chair next to his. He wrapped his arms around her. "Your smiling eyes get me every time."

Shortly after they headed back upstairs, as they turned the corner to the ER they saw a whole team of medical personnel in Angel's room.

"What's going on?" Aaron demanded.

"Dad, it's okay. They are administering the antidote. The team is there for precautionary measures," Brian relayed.

Aaron could see Maria holding Angel's hand. He bowed his head, held Eula's hand, and prayed.

"It's done," the doctor came out and informed them. "If all remains stable, we will move her to pediatrics within the hour."

Maria came out, "Her heart rate remained stable. She's talking their ears off. The swelling in her foot is dissipating, and the color is coming back. Praise Jesus!" Maria stammered.

"Mom, will you call Larry's cell and let him know? I don't want them worrying," she asked Eula.

"Yes, I will, but I need your phone. Mine is at the house."

Maria threw her phone to her mom. Eula walked outside to make the call and almost collided with Brian upon re-entering the room.

Aaron sat next to Angel's bed feeding her favorite cherry Jell-o.

"Well, that will keep her awake," Brian scolded Aaron.

"The nurse asked if she could have some. I forgot the red dye makes her hyper. Sorry," Aaron replied.

"No worries. She deserves it, but only this time, Pumpkin." Brian leaned over and kissed her head.

"Okay, Daddy," Angel replied.

Maria looked at the three of them, and her heart filled with pride at the kind and Godly heritage being passed onto her daughter.

"Mom, after they move Angel to ICU, I want you and Dad to go back to the Bungalow and rest. I'll call Larry and ask him to come get you," Maria commented.

"Oh sweetie, you worry too much. Why don't we see if there's a hotel close by? Larry and Adaline won't need to come back tonight. You and Brian can take shifts. One of you can rest at the hotel with us," Eula replied.

"Now that sounds like an excellent plan. I'll go make some calls," Aaron commented.

Brian talked to the doctor to see if there would be any permanent damage from the injury to Angel's foot. He was relieved to find out there would be only minimal nerve damage to the penetration sight. If Angel continued to improve, she would be released on Friday.

Chapter Six
SWEET VICTORIES

"Larry, wake up." Adaline shook him violently.

"What? What is it?" He rolled over to look at the clock. The neon numbers flashed in the darkness. "It's after ten, come to bed. We can talk tomorrow."

"I want to talk now." She plumped down on the bed beside him. "Do you think we should postpone the wedding? Obviously it won't happen tomorrow with our flower girl hurt? Maybe this is a bad idea. Do you think we should go back to the hospital? Larry! Are you listening?"

"No, yes, I heard you." He rolled over to face her. The moonlight rays cast a sweet glow about her face. "You're glowing." She cocked one eye up and semi-smiled. "I don't think they would want us to cancel the wedding, maybe postpone for a week. I can get an extension on the job at work." He cupped his hand like he held a phone and placed it to his ear. "Hello, Aaron, I know your granddaughter is in the hospital and almost died, but do you think you could hurry up a bit or give me extra time off?" He reached over and began tickling Adaline.

"Ha! Ha! Very funny! Now stop. I'm serious. You're going to hurt the baby."

"Yeah, right. The baby is the size of a pea or peanut. I forget which. It won't know the difference. You may pee your pants; that's all."

"You're such a smart-aleck sometimes." Adaline stood up and slammed the door as she walked out of the room.

"What?" Larry yelled. "Come on. I'm playing around." He changed into a pair of khakis shorts and a baseball T-shirt and went to apologize to his bride-to-be.

"Look, the Bible says to dwell with you according to knowledge." He muttered as he went through the house searching for her. He walked out on the porch and she sat sniffling on the swing. He sat next to her and put his arm around her shoulder, but she moved away.

Larry got up and knelt in front of her. "I'm sorry."

"Sorry for what?" She snapped.

"I'm sorry for not dwelling with you according to knowledge, for being insensitive, not taking our conversation seriously and being a moron. Need I go on?"

"Yes." A smile crept across her face. "You're forgiven, but you still haven't answered my question."

"I'm not sure how you want me to answer," he said.

Adaline stood up and pushed him to the side, stepped over him and bounded down the steps. "You are a moron, and don't follow me!" She demanded.

The full moon against the velvet sky made a lovely pathway down the beach. The waves lapping against the shore brought calmness and soothed her soul. She slowed her pace, took off her sandals and let her feet tingle in the white cascading ripples. Digging her feet into the wet sand brought back memories of her nanny playing with her at their beach house as a child. They would dig for hours in the lush white crystals hunting for treasures and build enormous castles, pretending to be swept away by a prince on a seahorse who lived under the great water's depths. It devastated her when Nana died, and she went to the boarding school at the age of ten; seeing her parents only on holidays or for brief visits made Adaline feel unloved. She wanted her child to know what it felt like to be unconditionally loved and genuinely cared for. Her marriage to Larry would solidify this baby being born into a caring and loving family.

∞

Larry ran his fingers through his hair and debated whether to call Aaron. After a few minutes of deliberation he decided to pick up the phone. "Did I wake you? I didn't want to disturb Brian."

"No, it's okay. He's been trying to call you. Angel is doing well. They moved her to ICU for precautionary care. What's up?" Aaron asked.

"I usually talk to Brian when I need advice, but his hands are full. I'm super sorry about bringing the wedding up at this point, but Adaline's upset with me. She thinks I'm being selfish and we should cancel having the wedding plans here. Maybe she's right in lieu of what's happened?" Larry proceeded.

"May I put Eula on the speaker phone? I think she might be able to help," Aaron questioned.

"Sure." Larry explained the argument to them and asked their opinion about the beach wedding.

"I think we need to see how Angel is doing before we make any determination. If she is released on Friday, we have the bungalow for another week, and the wedding can still go on as planned for the following Friday," Eula formulated.

"Larry, we may need to contact the designer for the landscaping job in Queen Creek to push the job out another week to be on the safe side." Aaron added.

"Sounds like a plan to me, but I wouldn't bring any of it up to Brian and Maria right now. Thanks for your help. I need to go find my fiancée," Larry remarked.

"Good night, Son. We'll see you later." Aaron hung up.

Larry grabbed a shawl hanging on the white painted coat rack. It reminded him of his grandma's old wooden one. She hung onto it for years because her husband made it for her out of recycled wood.

The couple was married for near fifty years when he passed away of a sudden heart attack. Grandma died a year later of a broken heart. They were the most faithful couple and best example Larry ever knew. He brought himself back to the present and grabbed a flashlight from the kitchen pantry.

∞

The crisp ocean breeze sent a chill down her spine and Adaline realized how far from the house her night dreaming took her. As she made her way back, the wind picked up and became brisk. The ominous clouds circled around the moon, giving it a translucent appearance. Her heart began to race a little as visibility became unclear. What was she thinking wandering off this far from the cottage alone at night? She reprimanded herself.

In the distance Adaline could see a small flicker of a light; it appeared to be moving toward her. A voice called out in the night, but with the rising and crashing waves and howling wind, she could not decipher the echo of words. She steadily moved toward it, hoping her love came to rescue her.

Larry couldn't see a blasted thing. The moon ducked behind a cloud before he saw Adaline's silhouette. He kept calling her name, and then out of fear he began to run down the shore. The flashlight flickered barely giving any visible light. "Adaline, Adaline," he yelled.

She nearly tripped over the end of the dock. Out of breath and exhausted, she sat down. Larry nearly ran right past her, but she hollered at him. "Larry, is it you?"

"Yes, this stupid flashlight is useless. Put your hand on the railing and we will work our way to each other," Larry instructed.

They worked their way down the wood until their fingers touched. Adaline collapsed into his arms. He held her close.

"I'm sorry. I'm an idiot." Larry conveyed.

"No, you're not! Don't say those words. I love you! Everything is going to turn out. I know we're supposed to get married. We'll work out the details later. Let's go back."

Larry draped the shawl over her shoulders and held her hand. He whacked the flashlight against his leg, and it came back on. His phone vibrated. It was Eula, but he wouldn't be able to hear her, so he let it go to voicemail.

When they made it to the house, Larry put water onto boil to make tea for Adaline and asked her to take a hot shower to warm up. He said a grateful prayer for their safety. After wrapping herself in a fleece blanket, she sipped on her drink. The hot ginger liquid made her feel soothed all over. They listened to the voicemail from Eula.

"Hope you two are getting some rest. I want you to tell Adaline not to blame herself or you for anything that is happening. Sometimes guilt or shame projects blame for other situations occurring. Reassure her, Father God doesn't work in that way. He loves you both. We love you too. Oh, before I go, Dad said his keys are in the cup holder next to the bed we were sleeping in. We need Angel's car seat from our car when you come in the morning. Ask Adaline if she would mind packing a little bag with a pair of clean clothes for each of us. Thanks Dears," Eula explained.

"Are you ready for some sleep?" Larry asked as he looked upon the lovely creature in front of him.

"Yes, I believe we are," Adaline responded as she leaned over and kissed him.

The next morning when Larry woke up Adaline wasn't next to him. He grabbed a sunflower from the arrangement on the table, a small bottle of ginger ale, a pack of saltines, and set out to look for his beloved.

Adaline sat cross-legged on the peer looking out at the waves cresting to the shore. Larry realized she never fully let him apologize the night before, and he waved the sunflower in the air like a flag in a sign of surrender.

"I already forgave you, wise guy. Peace offerings too. Thank you," she said as he handed her the flower and soda. "I don't suppose you stuck saltines in your pocket?" she asked.

"No, I don't think so." He fiddled around in his pockets, put his hand behind her ear, and brought forth a pack of crackers.

"Magical." She said, snatching them out of his hand.

"Here's the plan." Larry relayed his heart about the wedding and Aaron and Eula's suggestions. He sat behind her and enfolded her in his arms. "Jesus forgave us when we asked. He's not waiting to punish us for what we did. You need to believe it. The Enemy will bring stuff to make you doubt it. Do you understand?"

"Yes, I've never felt this way before. I'm perplexed and unsure. I've always been a strong Christian and thought I had a lot of faith. Now I just don't know. My dad's so hard and cold. I've never felt God to be the same, but I've never let Him down like this either. I'm struggling."

"Babe, you're one of the most steadfast people I know. You are human. You've got to forgive yourself. God already has. If he is upset with anyone, it would be me. I'm the head of our home. I should be stronger, but I'm learning and growing. I love you, my Shining Star. If it wasn't for your love for me, I might not be where I'm at in my relationship with the Lord today. I want to be the man God would have me be for you and our son. I will be because the Father is teaching me. Let's go pack up for the trip to the hospital." He squeezed her gently.

Larry and Adaline leisurely walked back to the cottage. She packed a suitcase with clothes for each of them, tucked Angel's blanket in with a couple of her books, a stuffed lamb, and followed Larry to the hospital in Aaron's vehicle.

∞

Angel's doctor removed the tube from her foot and moved her from ICU to the pediatric floor. She hobbled up into Adaline's lap, ready to hear a story book. The child winced when she put weight on the injured foot, but it didn't stop her tenacity. The nurse came in and put a walking boot on her.

"We'll change the bandage again later. After your lunch or nap, okay?" she said kindly.

"Okay, no nap," Angel retorted.

"Angel, is that how we talk?" Maria corrected.

"No," she held her head down, "Sorry." Her childish tone revealed she only half meant it.

The nurse patted Maria's arm. "Thank you. After lunch is fine."

When Adaline and Larry found their way to the child's room, Brian took Aaron's keys and asked his best bud if he wanted to go with him to gather a late breakfast for everyone. He placed the order online, so it would be ready for pickup when they arrived.

On the drive to the restaurant Brian started the conversation, "I wanted to talk to you privately. With everything and everyone being jolted from the accident, maybe you should postpone the wedding." Brian articulated.

"If you think so." Larry couldn't hide his disappointment. He barely spoke a word on the way back to the hospital. He listened to everything Brian shared with him intently, but only responded when a question was directly geared toward him.

When they arrived in Angel's room, she lay napping. Eula sat in the chair next to her.

"Where are the girls?" Brian asked

"They went to the cafeteria. Now shhh, she just got to sleep." Eula shooed them out of the room and quietly shut the door.

Brian and Larry found the ladies excitedly talking about wedding plans over coffee.

"What, I thought you would want to cancel after all that's happened?" Brian looked at Maria in disbelief.

"Oh no. Life's too short. It's going to be gorgeous. The weather is good next Friday and Saturday. I'll see if dad can push our departure out until Sunday evening," Maria shrilled.

"Thank you! Thank you!" Adaline hugged Maria, and Larry tackled Brian with a bear hug.

"Now that's what I'm talking about!" Larry eventually let go and gave him a high-five.

"We're in a hospital gentleman," an elderly nurse mused as she walked past.

"You're always getting me in trouble," Brian said as he punched Larry's arm.

The commotion did not faze the ladies at all. They kept right on talking. As the scent of eggs whiffed its way up to Adaline's nostrils, she covered her mouth and ran for the bathroom.

"When will the nausea subside?" Larry asked with a concerned look.

"It's different for everyone, but usually after the first trimester. Sometimes with boy pregnancies it seems harder," Maria answered.

"Boy? Isn't it a little early to tell?" Brian asked.

"Adaline told me the prophecy from the lady in the restaurant." Maria responded.

"This should be interesting. Would you like to share?" Brian questioned.

"Larry can tell you; I'm going to check on her. Take the eggs away; maybe leave her the pancakes please," Maria commented.

∞

Early the next morning the doctor came in to check on Angel; she spiked a fever in the night and it concerned him. He started her on a different strain of IV antibiotics, swabbed the wound area and sent it to the lab for testing. "No more getting out of bed for right now, young lady," he ordered.

She did not fuss, but laid her head back on the pillow in surrender. It was not long before she fell back to sleep.

"Brian, what is he looking for? I thought with the drainage tube out of her foot it seemed to be healing properly?" Maria's crinkled forehead and sad countenance revealed the depth of her anxiety.

"Yes, but there could still be an infection. It could also be her body's way of healing too. Let's not panic. We need to pray against MRSA, a strain of bacterium that can be serious. I'll call the prayer chain again. We need to get a handle on this now. We don't want any complications to her healing," Brian stressed. He tried to sound calm, but he knew how quickly this could become dangerous.

Once again Angel lay lethargic in her mom's arms, her little forehead beaded with sweat. Maria pushed the call button. "Nurse, her temperature is rising. I can feel it!"

The nurse came rushing back in and took Angel's vitals. "I'll call the doctor right away."

Maria started praying out loud; she didn't care who heard her. "Angel, you listen to me child. You are destined for great things. You are a princess, and one day you will rule a nation! The enemy can't have you! He tried to take you from me when you were a baby. He couldn't have you then, and he can't have you now in Yahshua's name! He can't win. He is a defeated foe. Father God, thank you for healing my baby girl in Yahshua's name. We believe and receive your healing.

Thank you, Lord!" Maria rocked her back and forth until she could literally feel the child's body temperature drop.

The nurse came in to give Angel a shot, but Maria said defiantly, "No, she doesn't need it now; the fever is gone."

"Ma'am it's doctor's orders, I must comply." The nurse pushed past Maria's arm.

Maria stood to her feet, "Please, take her temperature first."

The nurse huffed, snatched the thermometer and stuck it in Angel's right ear, within seconds it alarmed. Her mouth dropped open. "It's down to 99.0. How did it happen? It's impossible. I'll try the other side." She took again on left side. The reading was 98.9. "How did her temperature go from 103 ten minutes ago to normal?" She stood flabbergasted.

Maria carefully laid Angel on the bed and covered her with the sheet. "Let me tell you about the goodness of my Daddy."

The nurse stood and listened to every word, mesmerized as Maria explained the gospel and the healing that just took place. At the end of their conversation, the nurse bowed her head and accepted Jesus into her life.

"I've never seen anything like this. It's my first miracle. I hope to see many more. I feel new, and I don't realize how I could be loved this way, but I can receive it. Thank you!" She hugged Maria and walked out.

"Why is the nurse crying?" Brian asked as he walked in the room.

Maria recounted what happened. "I told Angel she is a princess and destined for great things. I'm tired of the enemy trying to take this child. I stood up to him, and I'm going to teach her how to now."

Brian stood speechless, starring at this fearless warrior before him. Angel ran no more fevers, and the white blood count was coming down at the last blood draw of the day. The next day the doctor released her from the hospital.

∞

On the way back to the bungalow Angel asked, "Daddy, may we go see the dolphins?"

"I don't know if it's a good idea today, Sweetie. Maybe we should all get a little rest first."

"Okay," she said sadly, "but when I was walking in the garden with Jesus yesterday, he told me to go see the dolphins," Angel informed her parents.

Brian pulled the car over to the shoulder. Maria and he turned around to face her.

"Honey, when did you see Jesus?" Maria asked.

"You know, Mommy, right before you were hollering at the debil. I was taking a nap. Jesus walked with me in His garden. His roses are prettier than yours. Real Big! Beautiful!" She clapped her hands together gleefully.

"And He told you to go see the dolphins?"

"Yes, yes He did."

Brian took out his cell and called the others. They rode ahead of them to prepare the house for their arrival. "Sorry folks. We've a stop to make. We'll be there in a few hours."

He grasped Maria's hand and squeezed in a silent gesture of thanksgiving. "We're going to see the dolphins, Princess. When Jesus talks, we always want to listen and obey."

She clapped her hands and squealed with joy.

"If you get tired, Daddy will carry you, okay? No throwing a fit or whining?"

"Okay!" Angel agreed.

The parking lot was eerily quiet at the aquarium. There were only a few cars and a black limousine.

"I don't know Brian. This is creepy. Isn't this their busy season?" Maria asked.

"Yeah, but its lunchtime, and look at the clouds. Maybe they scared people away today. Let's not be paranoid. After all, Jesus told Angel to come, right?" He laughed nervously.

"You aren't too reassuring," Maria said as she unclasped Angel's safety harness.

"Hold mommy and daddy's hand. On second thought, Daddy will carry you."

Angel started to protest, but remembered her sore foot. She caved in easily. Maria questioned the ticket lady, but the only answer she received was a special guest arrived today, so they were limiting admissions. The dolphin pool remained open.

Brian scoped out the building entrance and as far as he could see down the hall. There had not been any trouble since they closed the investigation surrounding Uncle Ron's shooting and the mysterious visitor. He did not anticipate any now, but he wanted to be cautious.

"Honey, I want to go to the restroom. Angel, do you need to go potty with Mommy?" Maria questioned.

Angel nodded her head yes. Brian lowered her gently to the ground. "I'll wait right outside the door." He did not like the long halls to the bathroom. They went into the main one. Brian leaned up against the door to the family restroom. All of a sudden it gave way, and someone yanked him inside, covering his mouth with an enormous hand. His fight or flight mechanism kicked in. He kicked, elbowed, and bit the assailant, but in his struggle something made him stop. He noticed penetrating scars on the back of the dark-skinned hand, then relaxed and said, "Rojomen, we've missed you my friend."

Rojomen released him and locked the door. "We must speak quietly. Is Angel okay?"

"Yes," Brian's face turned pale at the realization; this once guardian of his daughter might be there to collect their prized possession.

"Don't worry, my friend. It's not time yet, but I've critical news from our country. Her father is alive. My spies have found him. We'll try to recover him soon. The men who tried to kill your uncle and find you have gone underground. They are in hiding for now. However, there could be more trouble. We've increased our contacts in the States. You won't know who they are, but be assured they are looking out for you and your family. She is a beautiful little girl. You have done well. Thank you." Rojomen patted him on the shoulder.

"Honey, where are you?" Maria questioned in the empty hallway.

Rojomen nodded sternly. "No."

Brian responded, "I had to go to the restroom. Wait right there." He flushed the toilet and turned the faucet on.

Rojomen slipped a paper inside of Brian's jacket and whispered, "To help with your research."

"Thank you. Angel is kind and tenderhearted like you." Brian hugged Rojomen.

Brian slipped out the door and made sure he pulled it securely shut behind him.

"I heard the custodians talking, and there is a prince in the aquarium, hence the heightened security," he informed.

"Can I see the prince daddy?" Angel asked gleefully.

"Maybe, but for now let's go take a look at the dolphins," Brian winked at Maria.

Chapter Seven
Unveiled Forgiveness

The sun peeked over the pristine water shouting, "Its morning. Wake up!" Adaline peered through the open window blinds looking for a sign of the seagulls she fed on the dock yesterday. Their loud squawking appeared to her as a welcome call. She also hoped to get a glance at the family of dolphins out in the middle of the choppy waves. They would make a graceful backdrop for the pictures she wanted to take in the early morning light. Looking further down the sandy shore, she saw Eula and Aaron walking hand in hand. They had probably been up for hours she reasoned.

"It's perfect weather for a wedding. I pray Adaline isn't sick this morning, poor thing. She threw up four times yesterday while trying to make the flower bouquet." Eula noted.

"Yeah, I don't remember you that intensely sick when you were pregnant with Maria." Aaron replied.

The water danced upon the shore sending Eula scurrying to keep her feet from hitting the icy flow. Aaron laughed and sauntered around her.

Brian left to get everyone morning coffee and spend a few moments of quiet time before the bustle of the day. He needed to reflect on what he wanted to share at the ceremony as Larry added him in at the last minute to share something from his heart. The cake would be ready at the nearby bakery shortly after nine. It was a short block from the Lighthouse Coffee shop. He sat down to his caramel macchiato and opened his Bible to Ephesians. The prayer in chapter one, verses seventeen through twenty-one stood out to him.

Maria and Adaline prepared the flowers, punch, and finger foods. Larry entertained Angel as she still hobbled when applying full weight on her foot. Eula agreed to carry her to disperse the flower petals down the makeshift aisles.

Aaron and Eula worked on setting up the natural venue. The local church let them borrow a few chairs and they rented a rustic wood arbor decorated with white roses and feathers. Larry reached Pastor Stroke earlier in the week and he would be flying in and renting a vehicle to drive to their location. He said he wouldn't have missed it. Adaline's closest sister, Rose, would be driving in to represent the family. Uncle Ron phoned to see how far they were from his conference in L.A., and he too would be there. Aaron talked the owner of the bungalow into two extra days. They would have the wedding today, send Adaline and Larry on a surprise week honeymoon, and be out by Sunday night if everything went according to plan.

Brian's phone rang and he nearly dropped the cake as it teetered in his hand, trying to retrieve his cell from the deep pocket of his khaki pants. "Hello!" Brian answered annoyed.

"Sorry to bother you," Larry said.

"I'm trying to unlock my car door, and I almost slammed your cake to the ground."

"Oops. Sorry. Call me back, please. It's important."

"Alright," Brian laid the phone on top of the car, opened the door and set the cake on the floorboard. He did not want any mishaps if he needed to slam on his breaks. He could see that luscious masterpiece flatter than a flitter, as his dad use to say. He mindlessly got in, started the car and backed out. When he reached for his cell from his pocket to return Larry's call, he got a visual picture of where he left it, "Oh no!" He slammed on his brakes, "Not today, Lord!" Unfortunately his phone lay in a million scattered pieces on the pavement.

"There go all my contacts. What did Larry need?! Breathe, Brian, Breathe, One, Two, Three," he counted aloud. He scurried back into the bakery. "May I use your phone? Wait, our cells are all long distance."

"I'm sorry sir; I can't let you use our phone to make a long distance call. It's against store policy," the cashier said indifferent.

Brian explained what happened in detail and about the wedding, but to no avail. The young lady did apologize and directed him to a pay phone at the gas station. He could feel his temperature rising. He mumbled as he walked out the door, "Where is the compassion these days. I just spent $120 on a cake and they can't let me make a two minute emergency call."

He resisted the urge to slam the door on the way out and drove the five miles to the station. Everyone's coffee was cold now. Maria's chai would still be good because she liked it iced. Some surprise this turned out to be. Digging for quarters presented a challenge because Brian and Maria saved their spare change for Feed My Starving Children where they volunteered on occasions and intended to take Angel to help when she turned five. They wanted to build compassion in her for others from an early age. She already donated two toys of her choice to a Christmas charity every year from her collection.

His blood pressure rose by the minute. "This is ridiculous!" He slammed the car door.

A young man sitting on the curb came over to Brian, "Sir, may I help you?" The boy's tattered jeans, dirty shirt and black eye made Brian question the ironic nature of his statement.

"Not unless you have a phone I can use." Brian said gruffly.

"Matter of fact, I do." He handed him an old flip phone.

"Really, thanks, I sure needed your help this morning. You made my day." Brian felt bad about speaking rough to him and apologized.

"No worries. Take your time. I'll be over here." The boy sat back on his original spot and puffed on a cigarette butt.

"Honey, thank God you answered," Brian said exasperated.

"We've been trying to reach you." Maria started to scold, but noticing the tone in his voice stopped herself. "What's wrong?"

"I literally crushed my phone in a thousand pieces. Larry called me right before it happened. Do you know what he wanted?"

"I'm sorry. Yes, I do, but we are in the middle of preparations. I'll let him explain. Love you." Maria screamed for Larry. "Oh, sorry hon," she said as she passed the phone off to him.

"Hey bro. Pastor Stroke's flight is delayed. We've pushed the wedding to later this evening. The problem is we need some bamboo Tiki torches. Will you be able to go by the store and see if they have some while you are out? Sorry about your phone. That's a bummer."

"Sure, I guess it doesn't matter about the coffee at this point. Anything else?"

"Coffees?"

"Yeah, Surprise! Before nuptials coffee celebration, you sound pretty relaxed."

"Thanks, I'm sure they'll be fine. No, not really. Your wife has kept me so busy; I haven't time to think about being nervous." Larry laughed.

"Where are Mom and Dad?"

"I don't know. They left an hour or so ago, and said they'd be back. I'll put Maria back on the phone."

Brian could hear Angel hollering in the background, "Uncle Larry!" again, again, and again. Slight pause, "Pleasseeee!" She begged.

"Hi, babe, take a breath. It'll be okay." Together they did a karate black belt breath, inhaling deeply, holding ten seconds and then releasing slowly.

"See you soon. Thanks. Love you." Brian felt better already. Maria calmed his frayed nerves .

Brian told the young man thanks, handed him the phone and started to walk away, but something in his spirit lured him back. He turned to face the youth. "Son, what happened to your eye?"

"Oh, nothing really, just another run-in with my older brother, but it's okay. I'm not going back. I'm tired of his crap. Mom doesn't do anything about it anyway. I can't blame her; I guess. She's working her as…Oh, I'm sorry, she's trying to feed the four of us and keep a roof over our heads."

"Where's your dad?"

"I don't know, don't care either. That good for nothing drunk. Never did anything for us."

"This is abuse, Son. We should report it to the proper officials."

"No! It would hurt my mom too much! She does the best she can."

"Okay. Okay. I'm a doctor. Are you hurt anywhere else? Maybe I can help you."

"No, I'm okay!" The boy said vehemently. This conversation was getting way too personal, and the young man stood to leave, backing away from him, but stumbled and Brian reached out to catch him. The boy winced in pain as he touched his side to steady him.

"Hey man, I think you need to be checked out." Brian carefully expressed. This time he did not ask, but lifted the boy's shirt, and there were contusions up and down his rib cage around his back. The bruises appeared to be the size of a belt buckle. Now Brian became furious. His cheeks glowed a bright red flowing up to his neck. "Who did this to you?" Brian demanded.

"Doc, it's okay. Really. It's not the first time, and it won't be the last. I can handle it." He pulled his shirt down and away from Brian.

"Look, you could have some serious injuries you can't see. Let me call an ambulance or take you to the emergency room myself. I'll pay for it, if you're concerned about money."

"No man; I'm concerned about my mom, little brother, and sister."

"What if he hurts them in your absence?"

"I'll kill him!" The young man declared strongly. "My sister tried to protect me once, and he nearly broke her arm with a broom handle. I told him to take it out on me and leave them alone, so he has. It's my fault."

A police officer pulled up in front of the station to pump gas. Brian turned to walk over to him.

"Please, no." The young man quietly protested as he grabbed his arm.

"Go with me to the hospital and let them check you out." Brian persuaded. "If not, I'm going to talk to the cop."

"Alright, I'll go."

Brian took him to the hospital. They called his mother who left work to come sign papers for him to be treated. He had a severe concussion, broken ribs and a busted blood vessel above his right eye. The boy who turned out to be fourteen told the doctor he'd been in a skateboard accident and hit a pole, then skidded on the payment. He refused to rat on his brother. He could not bring himself to leave the other kids to the torture he received on a daily basis.

Brian's oath as a doctor could not allow him to sit idly by and let this monster continue to beat on this boy. The choice was no longer his to make. He prayed with the lad before he left and called the local child protective services from the nurse's station. He hated to do it, but justice demanded it and his oath procured it.

∞

"Where is he?" Maria paced back and forth in the kitchen. "He should've been back hours ago."

"I'm sure he's fine." Aaron tried to calm his daughter.

"We've less than an hour before the wedding. I'm going to dress Angel and fix her hair. Dad, can you help him with the lights when he returns? Thanks for the dresses you bought Angel and me. They're beautiful." She kissed her father on the cheek.

Larry fidgeted nervously with the clip on his tie. "Oh, heck. I don't need this. It's supposed to be casual." He threw it down on the small round table.

Eula approached the stand-up tent Aaron and Larry set-up earlier in the day for the men to dress in and hang out to keep them from seeing the bride prior to her walking down the lovely aisle the ladies created. The path wove a snake-like pattern between the few chairs decorated with purple ribbons, from the cottage steps to the archway. "Simplistic, but gorgeous against the backdrop of the ocean and the sunset behind it," Eula whispered. "Larry, how are you doing, son? Need any help?"

"I'm shaking; this clip on tie is ridiculous. Not going to wear it. Nope!"

"May I come in?"

"Yes, but you aren't changing my mind."

"Okay, I've got your corsage. May I pin it on? You look dashing. Let me see the tie." Sweetly laced in the ribbon of the corsage were the words, 'I'm my beloved's, and he is mine.' As Eula pinned it on the lapel of his shirt she said, "May I tell you a story?"

"Sure, do you know where my best man is? I don't think I'd be near as nervous if he were here."

"No, don't worry. He'll be here. Now listen. Once there lived a young lady in the mountains far away from the city lights. She lived in fear all alone. She'd been hurt many times by men in her life who were called to love her. One day in desperation she screamed out into the silent woods, "Who are you? Where are you? Why am I even here?" She lay on the forest floor weeping until she fell fast asleep. Not long into her rest, she began to dream. A man with kind eyes met her walking in the forest. At first she wanted to run, but something compelled her to stay. He asked, "Will you join me for a sit?" and pointed to a nice shaded spot on the flat rock in the crest of the wood's edge. She hesitated and spoke, "Only for a moment."

Larry spoke up, "We've less than an hour?" He looked at his watch.

Ignoring his interruption, Eula kept on talking, "The man revealed himself to her as forgiveness. He told her why he was created, about Jesus' death on the cross and how He wanted her to be free. She accepted this new friend and awoke from her sleep with a peace she never knew before. Buried deep in her hope chest at the end of her bed beneath a pile of blankets lay a Bible. As she read through the pages of her mom's worn leather cover book, finally she understood. Bowing her head, she received this new life it spoke of in Jesus Christ. Although her heart felt new, she still longed for someone to love and who would love her back. Many times she still felt desperately afraid.

One day a wounded hunter found her isolated cabin. Even though fear tried to grip her heart, she could not let him die. She carefully bandaged his wounds. He was a gentle soul. As he healed, they talked of life, their dreams, and aspirations. He also knew the Master, but called him Father. The young woman thought this was a beautiful intimacy she too longed for. This couple fell in love, shortened version. One night their love for each other grew much more intense like a fire burning out of control. They went further than they should, and well, you know the rest. The man, disgusted with himself, ridden with guilt and shame, left in the night in total remorse. The devastated lady decided she would take her life. She wrote a note, "I don't understand how something deep and beautiful can become terribly ugly. I can't take the pain anymore. Goodbye, my love. I'm sorry."

Far away from civilization, as she held the knife in her hand ready to end it all, a still small voice whispered, "Your pain is not greater than my forgiveness. You are forgiven. I died for your sin. I love you. You carry a child within."

With trembling hands she dropped the knife. As it fell to the floor, she kicked it away from her. There in the midst of the humble abode, she knelt and wept. She realized for the first time what forgiveness truly meant.

Larry could not hold back the tears. "Oh, but I've let Him down in so many ways. Adaline's the best thing that's ever happened to me. I don't want to disappoint God or her."

"God loves you. You're going to be a fantastic husband and father. You'll learn, grow, change, and make mistakes, but know this – your Father loves you and He's willing to forgive you. He'll always go to the very depths of Hell to bring us out. He already has. Always choose to run to Him."

"I will! Thank you!"

Eula hugged him and clipped his tie in place. "We love you, Son."

A car pulled up in the drive. Brian jumped out. Aaron met him outside.

"I'll explain later; right now we've a wedding to do," Brian said as he unloaded the car.

Uncle Ron drove up next with a tall, thin blonde by his side. "Well, hello everyone. Let me introduce you to my friend, Lacy. She smiled shyly and extended her hand.

Brian nodded cordially. He turned toward Ron and asked, "Sorry we are in somewhat of a rush. Do you mind helping us light these torches? I need to change." He then hollered into Larry's tent, "Sorry man; be right back." He darted into the house. Angel bounded into his arms before Maria could stop her vivacious child.

"Daddy, I missed you." Angel snuggled into his arm.

Brian shrugged his shoulders at Maria. She took Angel. "Daddy needs to change clothes now!"

"Mom, can you take Angel?" Maria yelled outside.

"Yes, Dear. Breathe," she said as she bounded up the stairs. Her mom stood there and counted to ten while Maria and Angel held their breath. Eula chuckled, "It's going to be fine, don't worry."

"Tell that to the bride. She's thrown up twice in the last hour and is beside herself. Never mind. I'll take Angel. You tell her 'the story'" Maria pleaded with her eyes.

"Delighted too!" Eula quipped. She tapped on Adaline's door. "May I come in?"

"Sure, but I'm a mess. Some bride I'm going to make." Adaline sobbed.

"Someone else told me the same thing. Well not the bride part, of course." Eula winked. "May I tell you a story?"

"Do we have time? I look terrible. My eyes are red and swollen from crying. "

"The wedding always waits for the bride. You don't look bad. It's nothing a little make up won't cure. You see yourself as terrible, but your perception is going to get a little makeover itself. Now I'll sit here beside you. We'll fix you up shortly." Eula conveyed the same story to Adaline she told Larry moments before. She took a damp cloth and washed Adaline's smeared face and prayed with her. "Do you feel better now?" She asked.

"Yes, yes I do. Thank you for sharing. I am forgiven. My baby is a gift, and Larry is too. We're going to be okay." She hugged Eula warmly.

"I'll have Maria come into help with your make-up and hair. Now, don't worry. Weddings never start on time. Pastor Stroke isn't here yet, but is on his way from the airport. This is your day. God wants you to enjoy every minute of it," Eula comforted. She patted her leg and left the room.

Adaline prayed, "Thank you, Father, for your forgiveness. Thank you for today, my special day, for my baby and hubby. Thank you for teaching us how to truly love."

Someone lightly knocked on Adaline's door, and she responded, "Come in, Maria."

The door slowly opened. "It's not Maria, but I'd love to help you get ready."

Adaline bounced up and down with joy as her big sister, Rose, entered the room. They grabbed hands and twirled around.

"Look at you, all grown up and a bride at that. Oh, I've missed you!" She held onto Adaline for a few minutes too long.

"I gotta catch my breath." She picked up her water and took a sip. "Will you put your cosmetology master skills together and help me looked marvelous?" Adaline asked.

"You know I will!" Rose got right to work. Adaline felt like the princess she'd always dreamed about in fairy tales.

The light shone over the horizon, dolphins danced in the distance to the music of Chris Tomlin's song, "Good, Good Father." The sun's rays cascading delightful warmth over the small gathering. Larry shifted from one foot to the other, eyes set on the door of the cottage, anticipation tugging at the strings of his heart. He longed to look upon his bride, the one who owned his affections and heart. He never thought he could feel this way about anyone, and now, oh now, the feelings rising up in him succumb anything he had ever known but always desired.

Everyone took their places. Eula hit the button on the karaoke machine to play the subtle instrumental of the wedding march. She gathered Angel in her arms, walking the child down the aisle between the two rows of chairs. The toddler's hand scooped the purple petals from the white wicker basket and threw them into the air. Then she dumped it upside down. The wind carried them and softly they floated to the sand, some drifting to the water's edge. This enticed the little girl and she wiggled out of Eula's arm, trying mightily to twirl around with her booted foot. She stopped halfway through and waved at her Daddy up in the front standing majestically by the groom.

The magical moment had come. All stood and she appeared, the bride, curls frolicking around her glowing face and flushed cheeks. Her eyes glistened with a new freshness and lips teased with a radiant, lustrous sparkle of red. Adaline carried a bouquet of white Easter lilies, a sign of hope and renewal, lilac interwoven with a touch of greenery tied together with lace from Maria's own wedding arrangement. Her strapless wedding gown fell delicately across the shoulders in floral lace. The figure-hugging form at the top flowed out to a pretty lace skirt.

Larry's shifting came to a reverent stance. His mouth dropped opened, and his eyes nearly bugged out of his head as Adaline sauntered down the aisle on Aaron's arm.

Rose stood as Maid of Honor and Maria as a bridesmaid, while Brian stood as Best Man. Aaron placed Adaline's hand in Larry's.

Rose sang a touching melody, "I Will Be Here" by Steve Curtis Chapman. Pastor Stroke led them magnificently, sharing his years of wisdom on love and intimacy.

After saying their tear-filled vows, Brian shared his heart on marriage before the exchange of rings. "Marriage is bigger than you. It's getting outside of you to love another properly, joining together in sacrifice, and caring more about your spouse's desires than your own. Jesus shows a picture of how to love when he commands the men to love their wives as He loves His church. He gave everything for us. A woman is created to respond to a man who loves her sincerely. The honor she is told to give to her husband comes easily when he obediently follows His Lord's path of love, to cherish, esteem and care for her unconditionally. The only greater intimacy and oneness that can be obtained is with Jesus. Men, let me tell you, intimacy begins when you enter the door of your home through communication with her. Women, your husband needs to feel respected in his home. Larry and Adaline, your marriage will be everything you put into it. It takes work and commitment to be the best it can be."

As the sun began to set, Adaline and Larry pledged their devotion and love to each other by lighting the unity candle. They knelt before the people who were the four pillars of faith in their lives and allowed them to anoint their heads and pray for them.

Pastor Stroke then announced, "Larry face Adaline; you may now kiss the bride, and save some for later."

Everyone cheered and applauded as Pastor Stroke announced, "I present to you, Mr. and Mrs. Larry Edward Ryan."

The couple took each other's hands and playfully dug their toes into the sand before running toward the house.

As everyone began to exist the beach, Aaron blurted out, "Wait, Wait please!"

Eula rushed to his side. "What is it hon, are you okay?"

"Would it be inappropriate for us to renew our vows? With everything that's happened in the last few years and Pastor Stroke being here, could we?" Aaron asked.

Adaline and Larry rushed back from the steps. In unison they yelled, "Go for it!"

Aaron and Eula joined hands and stood before Pastor Stroke. The rest of the family gathered around them to form a circle. Brian held sleepy Angel in his arms. The couple renewed their vows, quoting from memory. Ron stood in the distance snapping shots of the entire event. He looked over longingly at Lacy; maybe one day he could once again love.

Chapter Eight
SO FAR AWAY

As Maria snuggled under the puffy down comforter and flannel sheets, she felt the cold wrap around her feet like a thick London fog rolling in. She longed for her husband. He was the warm blanket for her soul and body. "When will he be home, Lord?" She whispered. The dark, silent night did not hold any answers. Bedtimes were the worst for Maria. She heard every little noise that crept in from outside, and the soft humming of the refrigerator or rugged sound of the heater. Her imagination brought her back to the comfort of his arms. She loved to slip into bed, stick her icy feet in the middle of his back and watch him holler. Even thought it was kind of mean, a tickling match always ensued. Then the security of his arms would wrap around her, and she would place her feet between his legs to warm them up. He loved it too and expressed this often in his conversations across the miles. She missed him terribly. Her heart ached for him to be home where he belonged.

Brian toured the hospital in Mexico and some clinics on his quest to help fight the ravaging cancer plaguing his patients. He was intrigued by Aaron's treatment process, which opened doors for him to investigate the Oasis of Hope hospital in Tijuana. He knew the ultimate healing for Aaron came from God's divine hand, but the success Dr. Contreras and his staff made in this field was outstanding and the evidence in the lives of their patience was undeniable.

Since moving to Flagstaff, Brian's job as chief oncologist at Flagstaff Memorial Hospital took him to two other leading areas in cancer prevention and cures, New Zealand and across Europe. He went on to publish his findings in the top medical journals.

Maria and Angel traveled with him to Europe, but stayed home this trip. Barbie, Maria's best friend, struggled with Lyme's disease and needed her help. It is one of the fastest growing and most difficult diseases to treat, leaving the individual in chronic pain with various debilitating conditions, affecting the mind and body. She helped them a lot with Angel during Aaron's sickness, and Brian understood his wife's desire to be there in her friend's time of need. He feared leaving his family, but hired a top security team to monitor activities around their home during his absence. He consoled himself with the last words Rojomen left him, promising to protect them.

Barbie received treatments at the Mayo Clinic. They were tedious, long, and the symptoms from the medication left her drained. Maria gave her great comfort and encouragement. Angel kept her spirits up with her childhood antics like a ballerina prancing around the house on her tippy-toes, a gymnast bouncing and rolling from the tops of each piece of furniture to the floor, using cushions as her mats. She would run through the house pretending to be a superhero or Veggie Tales character fighting off the bad guys with her doggie and baton with little evidence the child had a near-death experience. Even when Barbie could not get off the couch, she would be laughing until her stomach hurt. On the especially hard days, Angel would climb up in her lap and give her butterfly kisses, telling her, "I love you, Aunt Barbie. It'll be okay." Then she would take her sweet chubby hand and wipe tears from her auntie's eyes. Sometimes they would both fall asleep reading a story. It all ministered to the depths of Barbie's being, more than words could even describe.

Brian craved his family's company. He called Maria every morning and evening that he could and sometimes during the day when he was super pumped about a new finding. He drove with great ferocity toward cures like salmon swimming upstream, wading through the waters of countless fallacies concerning natural alternatives. This was not to say that some natural "doctors" weren't leeches, sucking blood from the desperate and hurting, but his research showed living evidences of natural cures, the most profound being the body's natural ability to heal itself, given the right tools, including the impact of food. He could not believe how few hours of training he received during medical school on nutrition.

The phone rang and startled Maria out of her dazed position.

"Hello. Oh honey, I almost jumped out of my skin. What are you doing at this late hour?" Maria asked.

"Hi, my love, I'm missing you, of course. Sorry for calling this late. I needed to hear your voice. We're traveling to a remote village in the mountains. We begin our journey today, and I won't have cell coverage for a few days. I don't want you to worry," Brian expressed.

"How many days will you be without your phone?" Maria's voice cracked.

Brian could hear the disappointment rising from her throat as she choked back the tears to be strong for him. He admired this in her. She cared more for him than anyone, and he felt a deep sense of gratitude.

"I know, I promised to be home by Sunday. This is a crucial opportunity, a once in a lifetime gift. I'll be gone another two weeks at least. Please, don't be upset. I'll make it up to you when I return. This is my last research trip out of the country this year, maybe for the next couple of years. The grant ends in January."

"We miss you. Angel asks for you every day. She's growing fast."

"I know." Brian's tone on the line was speechless as a knot formed in his throat. He tried clearing it.

"It's okay, Brian. Do what you need to. We're here waiting for you. We love and miss you."

"I wouldn't even be considering it, but this is the first time this island has even allowed visitors. You obtain permission from a chief. Otherwise it could cost you your life."

"Sounds dangerous to me," Maria responded.

Brian giggled nervously. "We've a whole entourage of guides and natives that know the terrain and speak the language."

"Okay, but you get back home to us! I love you!"

"I love you to the moon and back. I miss you too." Brian smacked his lips into the receiver and then growled as he gave a hug. "Good night, my love."

Maria hung up the phone and cried into her pillow. Angel came into the room and climbed in her bed. She snuggled up to her mommy and pulled Maria's face close to hers, taking her finger she wiped a tear that trickled down Maria's cheek.

"Daddy?" the child is wise beyond her years. She possesses a gift of compassion that knows no bounds.

"Yes," Maria replied.

"I miss him too," Angel stuck out her lip into a pout.

"So do I, my precious child." She kissed the little one's cheek and held her close until she fell asleep in Maria's arms. "Lord, thank you for this child. What would I do without her?"

Chapter Nine
THE ISLAND OF NEATORAMA

Wind whipped through the trees with such ferocity that palm branches were torn from their massive towering forms. They lay scattered on the ground, no longer connected to their life's source.

Brian contemplated how, when, and if the native warriors' makeshift shanty would hold up under the powerful force of the hurricane's mischievous gales. He came to the island of Neatorama seeking a medicine man who used the roots of a special tree to treat diseases among his people. The hospital would not grant funds for such an excursion. They said it was far too risky; however, they permitted the use of his vacation time to pursue his research.

He would willingly go to the ends of the earth to find the methods necessary to fight the deadly assailants stealing his patients' vitality. The only question lingering in his mind, "Would it be worth taking the risk of losing his own?"

Brian prayed silently at first, but as the storm grew closer, he prayed with great authority to bind the spirits of Death and Destruction in the hurricane's eye. He no longer cared if his warriors turned on him. He fought in the unseen realm of spiritual darkness to preserve life. To his surprise, the trail guide started translating his words with as much passion as Brian's declaration. The wind's ferocity ripped off the protective barriers from the roof. Rain poured in upon them like a mighty dam unleashed. Their voices were barely audible even though they were screaming the prayers now.

Brian vehemently proclaimed, "Peace be still in Jesus name!"

After an hour the storm ceased, and there appeared to be calmness in the air. The men stood wide-eyed.

Brian shouted, "Hallelujah!" and slapped his translator on the back. Spears were in his face and one just under his chin in the blink of an eye. He raised his arms high, then gently lowered them and knelt in a sign of surrender and a gesture of friendship.

His translator explained Brian's action as a greeting of victory among men in his culture. Smiles spread across their stern faces and they lowered their weapons. "We must prepare for the storm surge. It could still destroy us. It's too late to move inland or traverse the dense jungle. We make camp here tonight," the translator explained.

The men climbed up each other's shoulders and used Brian's tarp to secure the roof. They were agile and knew how to adapt to their environment. It was decided that two men would stand guard outside, and the rest would take turns sleeping at four-hour intervals.

Brian's fitful and restless sleep yielded no relief to his fatigued body. Even though the rain from the roof no longer filled the hut, the cold, wet ground seeped through his sleeping bag. He ached to be in his bed holding his wife and to cuddle with his little princess. In his mind he could see her panda bear wall chart moving up in inches by the hour. She took swim lessons at the Flagstaff Aquaplex, a multi-activity facility and ballet at Canyon Dance Academy. From the time she could walk, she loved to twirl around the house in her pink tutu up on her tippy-toes. Maria and Angel would sit for hours watching ballerinas and gymnasts in competitions or in the Olympics. He missed them terribly, and this primitive place had no cell or internet towers. After what seemed like an eternity of daydreaming, he drifted off to sleep to the light patter of rain falling from the trees.

Mumbling voices eased him back to consciousness. One eye, then the other slowly opened, "Where am I?"

"Daddy, Daddy, Daddy, wake up!" The shrieking voice demanded as it bounded up on his chest. He reached to pull his child close to him, but she disappeared from sight.

Brian woke instantly to the stark reality that he was only dreaming of Angel's voice calling out to him. He felt despondent at the concreteness that he had weeks to go before seeing her chubby chipmunk cheeks. It would take at least two weeks to fight their way through the intense jungle, meet the medicine man, and make their way back to the ships, barring any catastrophes of storm or beast.

He knew from experience that dreams could play important parts in the stories of people's lives. He hoped Angel's call to him did not signify they were in any kind of danger. Brian knew it could also be his own inner fears for their safety.

"Doctor, are you ready? We must begin our journey." It was more of a statement than a question from the thickly accented, ebony-skinned translator.

But Brian answered with a polite, "Yes."

"Okay, the packs are full. They'll be heavier than before due to the shells we carry. Bounty from the ocean."

"Why do we need shells?" Brian's questions could wait to a more appropriate time, but his curiosity got the better of him.

"The chief doesn't like intruders to this island, but he will see them as gifts from Mother Earth. He'll be much pleased. Also, the man you seek uses the crushed shells in his medicine. He isn't kind to strangers. He'll require a sacrifice, something of value to you." The translator pointed toward the men whacking their way through the thick brush, "Follow," he ordered.

As Brian hiked through the jungle, he pondered the translator's words, thinking about what offering he would give. He brought little of monetary value. The greatest gift he could offer would be his faith, which could possibly cost his life for venturing on unwanted territory.

A thick green snake slithered among the branches above their heads. Brian could see it inching its way toward them, but before he could react, its head fell to the ground with a mighty heave of a machete. Life ended in an instant. Brian stood with his tongue glued to the roof of his mouth, unable to speak.

"If it'd gotten any closer, you would be dead!" The leader snapped angrily. He muttered something in his native tongue and pushed Brian forward.

As the sun glared above the mighty cumulus clouds and the rays hit the detritus floor, consisting mainly of emitted vegetative parts, such as leaves, branches, bark, and stems, existing in various stages of decomposition, the shimmering droplets of rain danced on the tips of the luscious forest leaves and seared in the mind's memory the full vitality of heaven's canvas.

Brian's eyes were now alert, attentive, and on guard. He could see orange blossoms from the Canna jungle flame being formed from the nourishment of the water and sunlight sneaking its way through the trees. He knew this plant because of the tropical plants on display in the jungle arboretum he visited in Mexico.

He spied a large rock in the distance. "May we rest for a moment?" Brian timidly inquired.

"No! There!" He pointed to a mountain, then toward a darkened sky and toward the north. Brian's legs were not accustomed to the rugged terrain, and his shoulders burned from the burdensome pack. He could feel a blister forming on his heel from the wetness of the ground working its way into his boot.

It seemed like hours since they left the covering of the thick trees and made their way up to the majestic mountain's edge. The rain began to drizzle at first then coursed through the thick jungle canvas like a waterfall. The parka Brian pulled from his pack kept his upper body somewhat dry but felt smothering under humidity's veil.

The guide yelled, "There, we'll camp in the cave!"

Brian sat on a jagged rock inside the barely lit cave, took his boots off, and munched on a Clif bar. Maria sent a care package that arrived shortly before their departure consisting of nuts, protein bars and other light snacks. He offered one to the other six men, but they stared at him in disbelief and shook their heads. He peered out the cave entrance to a plant that stood brave and tall against the torrent of rain being gushed upon it. Brian wandered how it wasn't crushed under the weight. The single roseate bloom loomed above the fern green petals as if to say, "I will not be pulverized. I will weather this storm."

It reminded him of the Queen's Life guards in London he admired when touring the Royal Palace. They never wavered from their frozen stance, not even a smile, a flinch nor a movement of their bodies; they were set on their duty. At the time he thought they were cold and hard, but in reality Brian knew they represented loyalty and steadfastness to the finest degree, something he only began to understand.

∞

Adaline and Larry painted the nursery a pastel blue with chocolate colored trim. The walls were decorated with pictures of trains and fire trucks, collections from his years of fascination with emergency vehicles. In the closet the tubs held the toys in age appropriate sections. High above their heads a train made its way around the room on a suspended track, tooting its horn on the hour. When the lights were turned off, the engineer sounded off at one stop above the bed in soft, gentle tones, "Time for bed, sleepy head."

The pregnancy seemed to progress rapidly, and other than her occasional nausea, Adaline felt great. She completed her second trimester and confirmed their baby's gender, health, and size. He loved music, and when she could not get him to settle down, she would pop in a soothing instrumental by Beethoven or a lullaby CD.

Larry popped her on the butt with a towel, "You're supposed to be helping me hang this last shelf, not eating caramel ice cream and drifting off into LaLaLand."

"Ouch! Just for that I'm not telling you."

"Oh, come on. I'm sorry. Here, I'll kiss it." As he leaned over to smooch the area, Adaline jumped out of the way. He toppled over and hit his head on the dresser. Blood gushed from his temple.

"Oh my!" she yelled, ran to the bathroom, threw up, and gathered some towels. Larry followed her, holding pressure on the wound with his shirt. "That's dirty." She pressed a clean towel on the wound. After a few minutes, she demanded he let her take another look. "It's nasty. I think you should go to the ER."

"I don't think so. Where's my bro when I need him? Out gallivanting in some godforsaken country. Okay, maybe not forsaken, but out there. Where's our first aid kit?"

Adaline pulled the plastic container from the closet shelf. She tried to help him clean it up, but the bleeding would not stop and the Steri-strips would not stick. "Come on, hon, I'm going to be sick again." She handed him another clean cloth and bent over the toilet.

"Okay, I'll go, but only for you."

She drove to the hospital as he held pressure on the cut. The saturated towel did not keep blood from trickling down the side of his face. Adaline refused to look at him, even though he made jokes to get her to laugh.

"Don't be so serious; it's a little abrasion," Larry fused.

The doctor was as unimpressed as Adaline with Larry's lack of concern and wanted to keep him for observation. He stitched him up and gave a Tetanus injection plus antibiotic ointment. He asked, "Have you had any vomiting or dizziness?"

"No, I'm fine. Can I go?"

"Okay, wise guy. Sit up and swing your legs over to the edge of the bed slowly. Now place your feet on the floor, stand up, and walk toward me. No dizziness?"

"No!" Larry turned suddenly to wink at Adaline, and all went black. He woke up to the doctor standing over him, passing ammonia inhalants under his nose.

"Fine, huh? Let's get you back in bed. I'm ordering a CT of your head." He turned to the nurse. "Order a CT stat. I want to rule out any internal bleeding before I get you out of here." Adaline's face turned pale, and he looked at her. "It's only precautionary. I want to make sure he really has something up there working." He winked at her.

"Oh, I see, two can play at this game." Larry told him. He consoled Adaline, "Honey, I'm fine. A good jolt to my noggin, that's all. If I hit anything else we could be worried, but my head is hard as a rock." Larry laughed.

Adaline tried to share his optimism, but could not shake the eerie feeling growing inside her of something more serious. As they totted him off to X-ray, she rubbed her belly and talked to her son, "Daddy is going to be okay, sweet boy. Don't you worry now."

When Larry returned he had the attendant howling. "Hey babe, why don't you go get a bite to eat at the cafeteria? I'll be right here when you get back."

"Not a chance. This boy's been kicking my rib cage since we walked through the doors. He doesn't like it here," she responded.

∞

Brian munched away as the warriors stood tense, wide-eyed peering toward the tree line with spears extended. "What are they looking for?" Brian questioned.

"Shhh! See the rustling," he whispered. "Something is on the move. Legend tells of an enormous beast roaming this island. Few have seen it and lived to tell about it. It kills anything in its path."

Two of the men disappeared, one to the right and one to the left, outside the cave walls. "Where are they going?"

"There's a plant with the power to put the beast to sleep long enough for us to make our getaway. The men need only to anoint the tip of their spears with its thick juices and penetrate the tough coat of the creature's skin." The translator expressed in a monotone voice.

"I've medicine in my bag. It'll do the same if injected into the bloodstream," Brian spoke.

"There'll be no time; the spear is instant if thrown accurately."

The massive silhouette of the beast on all fours came into view barreling toward them with lightening accuracy in every jolt of its form, its glowing amber eyes and size like that of a Bengal tiger, and its elongated thick arms like that of a gorilla. Its mouth bore long, razor sharp teeth comparable to a mandrill.

∞

"The CT scan showed a small nodule above the injured site. The gash didn't penetrate it, but came close. You have a concussion. I would like to admit you and run a few more tests," the doctor explained to Larry.

"Doc, come on. I'm fine, really!" Larry insisted.

"Nonetheless, let's be on the safe side," Adaline replied.

"Oh, my word," Larry huffed.

The doctor nodded and walked out of the room.

"Call Aaron. We've a job to finish. I need to talk to him." Larry requested.

Adaline looked at him with poised hands on her hips.

"Please!" he snapped.

She dialed his number and handed Larry the phone. They talked for a few minutes. He turned to her, "Please, go home, eat, and get some rest. The last thing you need is to get sick."

"I will if you promise to behave and cooperate," Adaline countered.

"I promise, now go. I need some quiet time anyway. Maybe they'll have an MMA fight on."

She giggled and kissed him. "Bye. I love you."

"Never say 'bye,' just 'see ya later.' I love you too. Have I told you, you are the cutest pregnant lady ever?" he said smacking his lips.

She shook her head and walked out the door.

Not long after Adaline left, the nurse came in and told Larry they would be taking him for an MRI. The doctor wanted a better look at the mass above his eye.

A few hours later, Eula, Aaron and Adaline showed up together, Chick-fil-a in hand.

"Now something smells delicious. This hospital food is atrocious. Hi, you two," Larry's dinner tray sat barely touched on the counter.

"Let's pray, and we can dig in." Aaron said thanks, and prayed for Larry's healing. The baby started jumping around. Adaline squealed. "I'm telling you; this kid wants out. He punches like he's in a boxing match."

Eula reached out to feel his movement. "He's all over the place, an active child already."

"Yes, every time I smell food, he goes berserk."

"He must have a party when you eat." Aaron laughed. "He's definitely your child, active and always hungry." He gave Larry a high five.

They all started to get tickled and were in tears by the time the CNA came to check vitals. Larry nearly choked on the mouthful of spicy chicken he had salivating in his stuffed cheeks. Adaline handed him an ice cold Dr. Pepper. The doctor walked in with a forlorn look on his face.

"Is this your family?" he asked Larry.

"Yes, the only family I got." He introduced each of them. The doctor shook their hands.

"May they stay in the room for the MRI report?"

"Yes," Larry responded.

"Please, sit." He motioned the ladies to the two chairs, but Adaline stood by Larry's bed, grasping his hand. Larry gave her hand a gentle squeeze to let her know everything would be alright.

"The MRI revealed a somewhat bigger tumor than we expected. Larry you said you've had no prior symptoms until this accident. Is that correct?"

"Yes, sir."

"I've consulted with neurology, and they will be in to see you. We believe the mass is benign; however, these tumors are usually found in children and generally metastasize from the spine, if it is what I'm thinking. I would like to do an MRI of the spine to confirm this suspicion. A neurosurgeon will want to biopsy the tumor above your eye. It's a fairly simple procedure. The surgery will need to be scheduled right away before the mass grows. Then we can give you a more conclusive diagnosis. Do you have any questions?"

Larry shook his head no. For the first time since being admitted he was speechless.

"Will he be okay after the surgery?" Adaline started to choke up.

"Yes, he should be back to work within a few days, two weeks tops, as long as the dizziness clears up and there are no complications." The doctor replied and then politely dismissed himself.

Eula walked over to wrap her arms around Adaline. "I know it's scary, but it'll be okay. I don't want this to sound wrong, but I'm glad you hit your head, or they may not have found the mass until it caused serious issues."

"That's right. Praise Jesus. Thank you, Lord, for your protection and now for your healing," Aaron chimed in.

"Has anyone heard from Brian? When he'll be back? We've been caught up in preparing the nursery, and I've not checked in on Maria," Larry stated.

"No, it's been at least a week since Maria spoke with him. All we know is he is in some remote jungle somewhere. She's been busy caring for Barbie and taking care of Angel. Her hands are full. The treatment they are giving her friend seems to be working, but leaves her fatigued. She gave up her apartment a couple months ago. It was too much for her to take care of and is living at Maria's now. Mark, the guy, she'd been dating called it off when she started to get sick. Since the Mayo Clinic is here, and Flagstaff is three hours away, I suggested she move in with us," Eula answered.

"That guy is a jerk. We won't call Maria. She's enough on her plate, and I don't want her worrying about me. When we know something more definitive, I'll tell her," Larry stated.

∞

"We're going to die, Father, if you don't intervene now in Jesus name!" Brian yelled at the top of his lungs. It felt like a horror movie, death written in the temple of the beast's forehead. From above, he could hear one of men taunting the creature to draw its attention away from the cave. Momentarily, its eyes veered away from them and above the rock, a spear launched into the air and pierced the right shoulder of the massive form. It stumbled for a moment.

"Run! Now! Go!" The translator demanded and ran out of the cave, Brian hot on his heels.

"Sachwacha, Sachwacha!" the warrior screamed, and then everything drew silent, except for the heavy breath of their tormentor. The translator suddenly stopped and looked back. Brian plowed into the back of him, sending them both sprawling to the ground. The beast was dragging the man's limp body by his leg back toward the forest.

"We can't let this happen!" Brian ran back to the cave, pulled three syringes from his bag, and filled them with Etomidate. Judging the size of the animal, he did not want to take any chances and gave more than the maximum dose in hopes it would make the creature's heart stop beating.

"You'll never get close enough; it's not worth it. What about your family?" The translator argued and stood in front of him.

"Please, I must try; my God will help me. I've got to reach him before he gets into the trees!" Brian pleaded.

"I'll distract him." Together than ran as fast as they could toward the monster. Its injury and dragging a cumbersome body did little to slow it down. Brian went to the right, the translator dodged to the left, merely escaping one Kodiak claw's swipe.

Brian lunged forward, managing to get one syringe into the upper right quadrant of the chest, but the beast's raw thrust of the shoulder propelled him twenty feet into the air. The demon let go of his prey and charged at him as he hit the ground. The translator mustered his remaining strength, somersaulted into the air, and thrust his spear into the brute's neck. A piercing growl came from the interior of the being, nothing like Brian had ever heard. Its long arms and claws dug into the translator's skin. He writhed in pain.

Brian shook off the dazed feeling and quickly gathered the two remaining syringes from his pouch. From out of the trees, two screeches punctured the magenta night sky, simultaneously the two other warriors bounded up on the beast knocking the translator out of its grip, hurling him to the ground. Brian rushed in, gliding under its chest like going for home plate at the ball field. He thrust the needles deep into the area of the heart, pushing the medicine quickly in before he could clear the gargantuan body. It let out a sound like that of an avalanche crashing and collapsed on him. The two men on top looked like graceful gymnasts' as they flipped backwards off and landed feet first on the dirt.

At first they thought the beast crushed Brian, but its paw started rising in the air. They scurried over to help him out. Victory cries filled the atmosphere. Unfortunately, the first brave warrior's life could not be saved. He gave the ultimate sacrifice for his friends.

Brian, bruised and shook up, started treating the man's deep lacerations to his right leg and left arm. They made a travois to pull the translator on and ceremonially burned the other man's body.

As they stood while reverently watching the ashes fill the moonlit sky, the translator told Brian, "The men say, you are brave warrior, very brave!" He smiled big.

"We must move tonight. They'll carry fire on sticks to protect us. Need to get further up the mountain to the outskirts of the village. Protection is there. Many hours journey." He stood balanced on a pole, trying to hobble toward the others as if to say he did not need their help.

Brian put his hand on the shoulder of the man he now considered friend, "You are weak. You lost a lot of blood. You'll slow us down. Rest, I'll pull you. I'm strong." He flexed to show his muscles, and the translator laughed.

The other warrior came by Brian and slapped his back, pointed to the cot, and uttered his foreign tongue. The injured man immediately obeyed and climbed onto the tarp tied to the two sturdy bamboo limbs.

The winding path up the peak held treacherous passes, steep inclines, and briers with teeth-like claws that tore at Brian's clothes, ripping his skin. His breath became shallow as they made their way up in altitude. Falling, slipping, and sliding in the mushy ground made it difficult to hold onto the poles in his hands. Once he almost lost his friend off a narrow ravine. Finally, the leader doubled-back, eased his way around him, and took the polls from his weakened hands. As Brian took the rear of the pack, the other two men heaved the travois to their shoulders. They followed the thin mountain trail until it ended at a river.

The leader patted his shoulder and pointed to go across. Brian placed both feet in the frigid water. He swam with all his might in the direction instructed, but the vigorous current pushed him toward the rapids.

"Reach! Grab!" a voice yelled as a rope flew across Brian's head. He missed the first time.

"Oh, my God!" Panic began to rise in his chest and strangle the life out of him, paralyzing his movement, "Daddy, I've no fight left." He succumbed to the raging water. Suddenly an image of Maria and Angel flashed before his eyes. Hope surged within his mortal frame. He forced his burning legs to kick like a triathlon at the end of a race. The rope soared through the air, landing inches from his fingertips. A still small voice coursed through his ears, "Grab it, I have you, my Son." Like a sweet melody to his weary soul, the Father spoke.

Brian lunged forward, grasped the rope, and allowed his body to be pulled to the shore. He gasped for air, wheezing and coughing, his lungs burning like a brush fire out of control.

Somehow the tall warriors managed to carry the translator to shore. Their strong legs used to the water's temperatures and currents methodically stepped. The translator looked up to see Brian's face peering down at him.

"We are home," he said.

The men were ushered into tents. Brian worried about his friend. He lost a significant amount of blood. If only he could reach outside help. He mourned the loss of the first man captured by the beast. He prayed the translator would not become another casualty. He thanked God for saving him and the others. His heart yearned for home. He longed for his culture and body of believers to protect, to fight for their own and strangers as these mighty warriors did. They risked everything for him. When Rojomen slipped the paper in his hand concerning this island he knew nothing of the adventure awaiting him on this treacherous journey.

The creature they fought represented the ferocity of fear, destruction and death, much like the cancer he wanted desperately to rid from the earth. "Lord, how many people are tortured by this enemy? Please teach me how to fight and save them," Brian prayed. There would be no struggle tonight. He could not have stayed awake if he wanted too. His body demanded rest.

Early the next morning the guards summoned him at the crack of dawn. His body ached, but the men no longer responded roughly to him. The events bonded the men to a brotherhood. The chief beckoned them to the highest point at the crest of the mountain. The men bowed and lay the shells they managed to salvage at the foot of his ivory throne. Brian knelt before him in humble submission.

The translator beside him whispered, "Keep your head down. Do not look him in the eyes unless he speaks your name. Do not respond unless he directly questions to you. Show no fear."

The warriors spoke to the man of highest authority first, using signs and spears to express their plight. One of the men reached down and pulled Brian to his feet with his arm. He held his breath. He remembered the crumbled piece of paper in his pocket with words written he could not fully comprehend. The chief spoke Brian's name, and he looked up to face him. He was encased by black cascading locks, a dignified chin, piercing sable eyes and a silver nose ring. Two guards stood on each side of the majestic throne of their champion.

"They say you are brave. You were not afraid to fight the Sachwacha using your powerful medicine. Why are you here?" The man translated the chief's words carefully.

Brian explained why he ventured on this territory. He presented Rojomen's note. The stern face of the man relaxed into a semi-smile. "He saved my life once. I owe him likewise, so I'll preserve yours as he requests. You may meet with our medicine man within the next twenty-four hours. You must make it off the island by sunset on the third day. Another violent storm rises from the East. What sacrifice have you brought to the King?"

Brian drew a deep breath in, "In humility I kneel before you great one and offer the greatest gift ever given to me, at the risk of my life, just as your warriors risked their lives for me. My King gave his life for me and gave his all for mankind.

The Chief shifted on his seat and agitation grew on his crinkled brow. Spears were thrust into Brian's face. The chief uttered something, and they lowered their weapons. "I've heard of this king before. Go on."

Brian shared a parable of a wise shepherd who sacrificed his life for his sheep. A King who conquered the beast of death and the grave to rise again, one who would live and rule the hearts of his people forever, a good leader who served with honor, cared for his people with integrity and dignity, and fought with them in the thick of battle to conqueror their foes.

The Supreme Leader listened intently. Even though Brian could tell his contemplation by the look in his eyes and it reminded him of King Agrippa in the Bible, the chief sent him away from his presence, and his time began to tick away.

His heart yearned for this man leading his tribe to know the truth. Back in his tent the translator told Brian, "I want to know more of your King." He explained the gospel in more detail and led his friend in a prayer.

"I feel washed, like when we go down to the Crystal River and bathe. I no longer feel burdened or weak." The translator glowed with the freshness of new life. He looked on Brian's sad face. "You didn't fail, my friend. The chief will ponder your words. He'll never forget the white man who wasn't afraid to fight the demon that has plagued our people and stolen many lives."

Chapter Ten
Disturbing News

Barbie's emotions spiraled out of control like a spinning top with no boundaries. Maria did not know how much more she could take all alone. Her loneliness for Brian only magnified the way she felt. She picked up the phone and called her mother. No answer. She left a message, "Mom, I need you! Barbie's appointment is at 3 pm. Angel's dance recital is at 6 pm. I've not heard from Brian. I'm beside myself with worry. Please, call me!"

∞

The doctor entered the room, and even though Eula could see her phone vibrating she could not answer it. "Good news, Larry. There is no tumor on the spine, or any evidence from the blood work of cancer anywhere else. Did the neurosurgeon speak with you?"

"Yes, surgery is scheduled tomorrow at 11:30 am. What do you mean anywhere else? Before you answer, I'm also concerned about the anesthesia. I've not handle it well in the past. "

"First, we can't verify if the mass is benign until we get the biopsy report back. Why are you worried about the surgery, anesthetics in particular?"

"One time when Brian and I were kids, I rode my bike in front of a car. They did surgery to set my leg. When the doctors gave me general anesthesia I almost didn't wake up."

"It happened a long time ago, but we'll monitor you closely. You'll also talk to the anesthesiologists putting you under prior to pre-op."

Larry seemed satisfied with his answer, so he left the room. Adaline's face now flushed looked sternly at her husband. "You never told me about it," she said smugly.

"Never thought it important until now, you heard the doc, I'll be fine. Don't worry. Tell her," Larry looked at Eula.

"I'm sure everything is going to be just fine. Sorry, I really need to call Maria. Be right back." She smiled as she walked out the door.

In a few minutes she came back in to find Adaline lying next to Larry in the bed, his arms sweetly encased around her.

She blushed. "I'll leave you two love birds; Maria needs my help. Aaron will check on you later. Get some rest. You'll be home before you know it. Don't worry; you are praying, right?" She winked at them and walked down the hall, stopping by the nurses' station to ask them if they could give the couple a little time before disturbing them.

Adaline liked the instrumental music playing on the T.V.; the nature scenes and soft music lulled them both to sleep.

A clearing throat jarred them awake, "Hmmm. Hmmm. You two are resting well. I'm Dr. Clement, your anesthesiologist. I need to go over the prep, procedure, and post op medication for tomorrow. I'll tell you exactly what will be done and then answer any questions or address any concerns you may have."

They sat up and Adaline moved to the chair beside Larry's bed. He gave them a thorough evaluation of the proceedings. Larry told him of the previous experience he had as a child. He assured them of all of the factors would be taken into consideration. He would be monitored throughout the procedure, through recovery, and all the way to his room on the Neuro-intensive surgical unit.

"The surgery should only take forty-five minutes to an hour, barring any complications, which we don't anticipate in this case. You will be in recovery one to two hours. It's normal to feel groggy and nauseous when you wake up. After you are awake and stable, Adaline or another family member may sit with you. Do you have any further questions?" he asked.

"Yes, why does he need to go to ICU?" Adaline fearfully expressed.

"It's standard procedure; everyone having brain surgery must go to the ICU for twenty-four hours to be monitored, a precautionary measure to clear the patient of any seizure activity. It is not uncommon for a patient to have a seizure post-op."

"Seizure!" Larry exclaimed. "First mention of this possibility."

"I assure you; it doesn't happen often with a surgery as minor as yours. We have medication to stop it immediately, if it does." He finished answering their questions, bid them good-night, and shut the door behind him.

"I'm sick of these professionals acting nonchalantly about this. No big deal. It happens all the time. You're just having brain surgery; that's all. Why are you upset? Well, I'm sorry. It's still surgery on your head!" Adaline raved.

"I know, but they don't consider it major surgery. My head is like a rock. It'll be okay. Let's pray. I want you to go home and try to rest, or stay with Eula and Aaron tonight, okay? Please." He gave her the puppy dog eyes.

"Okay, I'll go to their house. I like her daybed anyway; the cushions on it fit nicely between my prego belly and legs."

Larry called Aaron and asked him to pick up Adaline. She finally conceded to go before visiting hours were over. She kissed him before leaving to meet him at the front of the hospital. The only reason she agreed to leave was the precious cargo she carried inside, she knew Larry needed quiet, and that he shouldn't have to worry about them too.

At 6 am the nurses prepped Larry for surgery to remove a right frontal lobe tumor. They shaved the area where the incision would be made to peel back the skin revealing the mass. The nurses were about ready to whisk him away when Adaline, Aaron, and Eula came in at

8:00 to pray with him. "Make it quick; we need to get him to the pre-surgery holding area." one of the nurses clad in blue scrubs voiced.

"I thought they were taking you at 9:00?" Adaline smartly remarked.

The nurse did not respond, but turned and walked out.

"Yes, we will" Aaron respectfully responded.

Adaline's cheeks turned red.

"It's okay, honey," Larry reassured her. "The sooner, the better; let's get this over-with so we can get on with our lives."

After prayers were finished, Eula and Aaron stepped out to give them a minute of privacy. The couple kissed and hugged each other. Larry smiled and rubbed her belly, talking to the baby inside. "Daddy, will be back soon, fit as a fiddle."

Adaline laughed, "Where did you come up with that?"

"My grandfather used to say it."

The nurse abruptly pushed her way past them. "It's time now," she stated. "You can go up to the first floor surgery waiting room."

"I love you!" Adaline expressed, as she wrapped her arms around her chest.

"I love you more. See you soon." Larry blew her a kiss.

Tears trickled down Adaline's cheeks. Eula gathered her into her arms.

"One of us must stay in the surgery waiting area. Why don't you two go grab some coffee and a bite to eat, my treat? When you get back, I'll go." Aaron tossed his wallet to Eula as he walked away whistling, "Amazing Grace."

"I guess there was no room to say no there," Eula chuckled and grabbed Adaline's arm.

The surgery seemed like it took hours to get started. One saving grace was the hospital had a monitor reading each stage of the surgery process, Pre-surgery, In Surgery, Post and Recovery. Volunteers assigned at the reception desk would periodically call for a member from the patient's family and give an update. The waiting area was packed in like sardines, family and friends lingering to hear news of their loved ones. After each procedure ended, a patient's name was broadcast over the intercom and the family was directed to a small room to receive the surgical report.

Some families came out celebrating victoriously with smiles, hugs and cheers, others with tear-streaked, solemn, or angry faces. Still others had a look of shock and bewilderment, not quiet knowing how to process the information they had been given.

Adaline stood strong in the belief Larry would be fine and refused to get on the train of thoughts racing around in her head. She knew the devil loved to play on the emotions stirring around in the soul, planting thoughts of fear and doubt like weeds in a garden. Instead, she focused on praying for the people around her.

When she felt restless, she would walk the hall, meander through the sea of visitors, and chat with the volunteers. It's at those moments, she would take careful notice of the eyes of those waiting, praying for any who appeared distraught or scared. In the bathroom she held a middle-aged woman whose sister received the diagnosis of malignant brain cancer, letting her release grief-stricken sobs and comforting the poor thing. "It's never over until it's over. May I play a song for you on my phone; something to encourage you not to give up? The doctors aren't bigger than God, and they don't know everything." The lady shook her head, yes.

Adaline handed her the phone, and the words reverberated off the bathroom walls like echoes in a canyon; a music video by Mandisa called, "Overcomer" filled the air.

"That's beautiful. Thank you. Will you write down the name and artist for me? I would like to show it to my sister."

"Yes. We'll have to go out to my purse. There is someone I'd like you to meet." She interlocked her arm in the lady's to steady and support her. They walked together to where Eula and Aaron sat.

"Aaron, Eula, this is Marcela. Will you tell her your story?" Adaline asked.

"Oh, I'll have to go soon. They'll be taking my sister to ICU. If it won't take long, I guess I can sit for a minute," she said uncomfortably.

Adaline patted her arm. "I'll listen for her name and write the information about the video on the back of my husband's business card. If you ever need to talk, call me."

"Okay, thank you," Marcela replied.

Eula motioned for her to have a seat beside her. She hesitantly lowered herself down, unsure of this scenario. Aaron shared a shortened version of his experience with cancer, death, and healing. Her eyes lit up brightly. Before anymore words could be exchanged, her sister's name echoed over the intercom. She stood abruptly and made her way to the information desk.

"Remember, don't ever give up! We'll be praying for you and your sister!" Aaron shouted after her.

Glancing back, she smiled and gave them a wave. She yelled back, "I do believe!"

Adaline waved a childlike goodbye. She reveled in God's reassurance of His presence in the most unlikely of places by allowing her to show someone else compassion and love in the midst of their pain.

"Family for Larry," rang out over the speaker. "Room one."

Eula, Aaron, and Adaline settled in the black leather cushioned chairs in the humble room. One slender lamp with a white shade lit the place, casting a shadow off the wall. This area definitely relayed its meaning, for short-term usage. The walls hung with a looming cloud of coldness and sadness. The matter-of-fact stance of the surgeon matched the dreary surroundings perfectly.

"We removed the entirety of the tumor. It appears benign; however, we'll know more once the results from the biopsy are in. A chemo-oncologist will be contacting you. These types of tumors are normally metastasized from the spine and generally a childhood form of cell mutation. The MRI revealed no growth on Larry's spine," the surgeon stated.

"I don't understand. Chemotherapy seems pretty dramatic for a benign tumor." Wells started forming in Adaline's eyes.

"The chemo is to ensure there is no further growth on the brain. We'd like to do a PET scan. It'll check his full skeleton, highlighting any areas of potential tumor growth. We've come a long way in treating patients with chemotherapy. Now a patient takes a pill once a day for a prescribed period of time; there are few side effects. In fact, most people have no problems at all and do very well. The specialty pharmacist will be calling you to set-up insurance and payments plans, if needed. We'll give his surgical sight two weeks to heal and then start treatment. Your oncologist can answer any further questions you may have."

The mother bear in Eula had enough with his pompous attitude. She could no longer contain it. "Wait a minute! Do not place orders for medication until we talk to the patient."

He turned to Adaline, "We'll discuss the options when your husband comes out of recovery and is up in ICU within the next few hours. Good day." He bolted out the door before any more confrontations could occur.

"How dare he?" Eula buried her head in Aaron's chest.

"We won't do anything Larry doesn't want to do. We don't believe it'll come back anyway. I'm sure it's their standard practice, like every patient is the same and bodies react exactly alike," Adaline comforted her.

"Why is he going to ICU?" Aaron asked.

"Apparently it's protocol after brain surgery for twenty-four to forty-eight hours," Adaline answered. "I want to buy him a treat on the way up to the room. He loves iced coffee with plenty of syrup, topped off with whipped cream."

"I wouldn't do it just yet. I'm not sure the nurses will allow it there, at least not until he is on a regular diet," Eula piped up.

Someone lightly tapped on the door, then opened it gingerly.

"Maria, what are you doing here? Where's Angel?"

"Barbie is feeling better and took her to the park. I've not been here for ya'll, so here I am. We came down to stay with Mom while Brian is gone, so she had to tell me what was going on." She said, glancing over at her dad. "Barbie's treatments at Mayo are making the commute back and forth difficult. Plus I miss him something fierce. Being around my family makes me feel his presence, even though he isn't here. Sounds weird, I know," Maria replied as she hugged Adaline.

"Have you heard from him?" Aaron questioned.

Maria hung her head, "No, I'm worried sick. It's been almost two weeks, but look you've enough to worry about. How's Larry?"

"He's good. Surgery went well. They removed the tumor. He should be back on his feet in no time. A boulder couldn't hold that man down." Adaline chuckled.

They made their way to the ICU hall. Everyone wanting to see a family member called in on a speaker phone/camera and waited until they were buzzed in by the nurse, or security came at designated hours and let people in with their photo ID cards. There wasn't a waiting room nearby, and the standing could be an hour or more as visitors came and went. You could not take a backpack or purse in; therefore, an individual who was alone would need to leave their items in a locker three floors down or in their car in the parking garage.

No food or drinks were allowed. Aaron experienced making the long trek back to the car to retrieve items twice during the next couple of days as it was easy for the ladies to forget their ID's in their purses.

Larry made a speedy recovery and came out of anesthesia much better than he feared. He walked around the nurses' station twice the second day and moved to a regular room early on the third day. He was flabbergasted when the oncologists came in to discuss his "options" for treatment because he was under the impression the tumor would be removed, and that was the end of that. He politely told her he wasn't doing anything until he consulted his best buddy, top oncologist in the field. The evening of the third day they released him from the hospital.

"Oh, come on. I can walk out of here," Larry insisted, his pride latching hold of his heart.

The polite volunteer said, "No, it's hospital policy. Do you want to get me fired?" he harassed back.

"Well, of course. No, I'm kidding," Larry jested.

Chapter Eleven
SEARING VIPER

The medicine man's rough appearance threw Brian a bit, smooth white bones penetrated his nose, upper lip, and just below his mouth. His matted beard a mixture of grey and black fell just beneath his chest. Doctors in the Western culture would get ostracized for such an appearance. He tried to stay focused on his purpose for being there. Albeit apprehensively, the rugged man showed Brian the mixture of crushed shells, flower seeds, and tree roots.

A patient with severe pain and a distended stomach was ushered in. The medicine man added some of the potency to a wooden cup filled with water and grunted for her to drink, pushing it toward her mouth. She gagged but managed to drink it down. Then he shooed her out of his dwelling.

"That's it? No exam? He just hands them this concoction?" Brian gawked in disbelief. His temper started to flare. They were running out of time, and he needed more answers. "Where do the plants come from? How can I experiment with them?"

The translator tugged him outside the door made of animal skin. "Peace, my friend. You may not get all of your answers this trip. If they feel threatened in any way, you will not make it off this island. Grace as you explained to me is extended, but only as they see fit. You are lucky to have any access; you are the first."

Brian took a walk to calm his frazzled nerves. The darkness of this place far outweighed any beauty it held in his eyes. "Daddy, I don't understand why you brought me here, if I can't get the answers I need, but I'll trust you."

He walked back into the humble dwellings; the dirt floors, palm leaf roofs and bamboo walls reminded Brian of the blessings waiting for him at home and how thankful he was for them.

"Now, you do it!" the translator demanded as he spoke for the medicine man. He wanted Brian to formulate the mixture after seeing him do it once. His skillful hands and sharp mind did exactly as instructed. His friend shared a crooked smile; however, the man unimpressed, pushed them out, yelling, "Go find more!" in his native tongue.

Somehow even Brian understood this not to be a friendly request.

"We've less than two hours of daylight. We must act quickly as we leave at daybreak per the chief's orders," the translator cautioned.

"It's impossible. No, no, it's not," Brian stopped himself. "We must find the root and petals. The broken shells are in our tent. You know the makeup of the island. Where do we begin?"

"Not very well, it's been many years since my return. Look." The translator pointed to a man walking their way.

One of the warriors approached; the man Brian saved knelt before him. "I'm indebted to you. My life is yours until I repay you by saving yours," the translator explained.

Brian started to say no, but his friend silenced him by putting his hand to his own throat making a slicing sign. He could not refuse. This man must fulfill his oath or kill himself.

"Okay, ask him if he can help us?" The translator explained to the experienced warrior their situation. He took his spear and began leading them. They walked for what seemed like hours to the northeast side of the dormant volcanic mountain. A cascading waterfall embraced its upper banks and flowed down the side of the steep crest. The servant led them behind the waterfall where a gorgeous flaming bush bloomed, its roots running through the rock and into the water's stream. As Brian reached for the flower's petals, a viper pierced its razor sharp teeth deep into his skin. Immediately, his head began to spin. In an instant, the warrior yielded his machete and cut off the head of the vicious snake. Then he took the sharp edge of the knife hanging from his side and sliced into Brian's thenar space, the area between the thumb and the index finger. He began to suck the venom from the blood and spit it to the ground. Brian sweated profusely as the translator lay him to the ground, tearing material from his own clothing to wrap around the wound.

The warrior pulled the petals from the bush, "I must cut some of the root. Stay here." He left the entrance of the water wall. Chills coursed through Brian's body as fever raged from within, his body's immune system attacking the foreign liquid enemy mixed within. The last thing he saw before losing consciousness was the last glimmer of the sun's rays slicing the waterfalls current. He dreamed, and the translator prayed to his new God.

∞

Light glittered all around Brian, more intense than he ever knew. He walked toward a gate made of shimmering gold with pearls laced throughout. There stood a man, hair and beard Clorox white, a flowing gown with a blue sash from his right shoulder to his feet. A pedestal of gopher's wood held a large book floating in the air above it. This feels a lot like what I remember the Bible talking about Heaven, he thought. In a mini-second the man responded to his impression.

"Yes, you are at Heaven's gates. If your name is here, you will be ushered into the next gate where you will be given a new body and name by our Master. Brian, I know yours is written here because I've watched you for years. You are a good and faithful servant of our Lord. He says enter into His rest."

A man appeared with glowing eyes, soft skin, and a robe with an embedded purple sash, reading King of Kings and Lord of Lords. "I would like to walk with you to my Father's throne before we proceed further."

As they approached the throne, Brian could see jewels, finer in splendor than any he had ever known, the intense green of emerald, the translucent gold of topaz, the deep shimmering onyx, the rich deep purple of amethyst, transparent red jacinth and olive green chrysolite. There were colors from dusty pink to skylight blue to aquamarine.

He knelt before the magnificent ivory throne with a hallo of fire around it. The angels were singing, "Holy, Holy, Holy are you Lord God Almighty!" Jesus' piercingly gentle eyes looked down upon Brian and lifted his face toward him. The Father gently held his hand out to him. He reached out for it, and his mind flashed back to a time at a summer camp when he knelt and gave His life to the Lord. On the wall was a picture of Jesus holding a child in His lap. Love exuded from Abba, and a thick transparent cloud surrounded them.

Brian felt as if his heart would explode. Overwhelmed at the majesty, he crumpled to the lap of His creator. "I've a special job for you here. My son gives everyone who comes to Heaven a new name, chosen from before the foundation of the world, specifically for them, and each person who has accepted my Son receives a new body when they enter our kingdom. Your whole life you have given to see healing come to others. Now you will be at the portal of heaven to see them made whole and dress each one with a new body. Your new name will be…"

Brian started shaking violently and awoke drenched in perspiration. He lay in a tent covered with a blanket. Tranquility filled his soul, a peace that passes all understanding vibrating throughout his body to his very core.

The camp bustled outside; he could hear the translation of a leader shouting commands, but he felt a joy bubbling from within like a spring underneath the earth's surface searching for a release. The darkness inside the tent let Brian know the night penetrated their ticking clock.

The translator peeped his head inside the hut. "Hi, my friend, you live," he said joyfully. The man explained to Brian how the warrior found the root, applied it the wound, and carried him on his back through the rocky mountain terrain. Through the rain he stood strong and never lost his footing.

"It'll be daylight soon. The urgency for us to leave is here. If we don't leave as ordered, we'll not make it off this mountain," his friend advised.

Brian desperately wanted to protest. There was much more he needed to know, the amounts and strengths of the medicine, did the chief accept Jesus and how would he know what to do with the information partially given? But then he recollected the dream and relented.

His friend looked sternly into his eyes. "You did more than you'll ever know. Do you think you can stand?" He took Brian's arm and helped him up, but in his weakened and dizzy condition, he toppled to the ground. "It's okay." The translator motioned for the warrior to come inside and gave him instructions. "He must carry you. There is no time to make and pull a travois. It would take too long to get down the mountain. We gave you the potency, but it takes time to overcome the poison. It's imperative we clear the range before sunset to make it off the island by the third day. Pray our boat is still intact and that our strength holds out. The other men aren't allowed to accompany us on this journey. There is threat of war from a faction which broke off from the tribe. The chief required all able bodies to remain, except for the servant who vowed to save you and me, your humble guide."

"We'll make it," Brian half-stated and questioned.

"Nothing is impossible."

The strong warrior knelt his weary body before him. Brian cringed at the scrapes and bruises he endured carrying him before. His heart melted at the courage and loyalty of this brave man. The translator helped him climb on his back. Then he took Brian's belt and looped it around them. He then tied off their backpacks to his shoulders. Each man carried a spear as they began their descent.

Brian fought back tears. His battered body felt nothing compared to the humility flooding his soul.

The raw emotions of this integral trip through the curvy, rocky trail ripped through his mind like a massive mudslide, tearing at the core of his being and beliefs. The thoughts did not tear at his faith, but left room for solid reflection on how to stand faithful and loyal to the soldiers in his own army. At first, a sly demonic force whispered, "You failed. You're a failure. You can't even walk down this mountain; someone else is carrying you. What have you gained for all your trouble? Nothing." He knew part of the hallucination came from his body fighting the toxin flowing through his bloodstream. He fought to hang on to the reality of the truth he had been given. "Devil, you're a liar, flee from me, in Jesus' name."

The warrior stumbled multiple times with the heavy weight he carried, but he stood like the mighty summit. He did not stop or waver in his downward goal. They made it off the mountain to the cave where they previously made shelter. Brian terrifyingly looked over to where the massive creature once lay.

Bewildered, he called to the translator, "What? How could it be?"

The guide unhooked Brian, and the servant lowered him to the ground. "There'll be no fire tonight. Someone might've taken it for hide, food, or it may still be alive. Hopefully we'll not find out."

The servant warrior scavenged for food and guarded their camp the rest of the night. Brian did not understand how he still stood. He remained useless to help. By the next morning, his strength began to return. He definitely could not sprint, but the dizziness disappeared and his color returned. They headed for the ocean shore through the path cut by the machetes on their trip in. When Brian's steps started faltering, the warrior demanded he climb on his back. Their journey came to an abrupt end halfway through the trail as spears encircled them.

Brian sighed, "You've got to be kidding me. Father, get us off this island, in Jesus name!"

The servant lay Brian to the ground, and stood over him with his spear as a protective barrier. The translator also extended his weapon. "Brothers, we mean no harm; we must get off this island. Let us pass peacefully. No one need die today." The guide translated the warrior's words.

Out of the jungle appeared a handful of tribal men. Brian dared not speak a word. One of the men pointed to the packs on their backs; they threw the bags to them. The satisfied group disappeared into the thick greenery.

"Wait!" Brian pleaded. "Everything is in the pack, my notebook, journal, phone...everything," he said despairingly.

"Shhh, we made it out with our lives! Quickly, go!" The only thing left was a sleeping bag because Brian lay over it when he was lowered to the ground.

The sun shone hot in the late afternoon sky as they made it to the shore. Brian knelt in the sand and bowed his head. He thanked God for their safety and the two boats in front of them still anchored to the towering tree. The other boats were smashed against the rocks across the crescent sand bank. Now they would need only one, but how would they survive with no food, water, or protection from the scorching rays above? If the chief correctly predicted the storm's arrival, they would need to make it back to the offshore ships by morning, assuming one would still be there, considering they were several days behind schedule.

He bowed himself before the mighty warrior servant and asked the translator to decipher his words. "You are released; you've saved my life these three times. Please go back to your people."

"Thank you. No, must get you to safety," he said as he pointed to the barren ocean, nothing but water as far as they could see.

"Your people need you. Please, you are free from this debt." Brian took the chain that hung from his neck. "Peace." This gift signified the end of his commitment, a parting gift. The translator relayed the message and Brian's deep appreciation for his brave sacrifice. "My God will get us there."

The puzzled warrior asked of this God Brian spoke of. The translator quickly explained the gospel using the sacrifices the man had made to save their lives.

"Me know this God?" he asked.

"Yes. Yes." They led him in a prayer of salvation. Brian once again told the translator to express his release. This time he accepted the gift, tore his tiger tooth from his neck, and handed it to Brian as he reverently bowed, saying, "You must go." He disappeared into the covering of the trees.

The clouds swirled above their heads, dark and ominous. The waves were choppy. They rowed hard against the current pushing them toward the shore. Brian prayed out loud and used the air from his diaphragm to sing the song of Moses, "I will sing to the Lord, for He has triumphed gloriously! The horse and the riders thrown into the sea! The Lord, my God, my strength, my song, has become my victory. He's my God, and I will praise Him. My Father's God, and I will exalt Him!"

A wave nearly toppled them over, but Brian kept singing. He refused to give up. His family's picture forged in his mind drove him forward with great determination. Their arms burned, and sweat poured from their clothing. After seemingly hours, and far from being able to see the shore for the clouds now towering over the waters, Brian fell exhausted to the side of the boat.

The translator continued to row. "God will hold off the storm until we reach safety," he said defiant against the tempest.

Brian picked up the oar as he imagined holding Maria and cradling his little girl. The moon reflected off the salt water as it peeked between the nimbus cumulus clouds. He thought it looked to be smiling at them. Now they would only have the glow of the moon to lead them as they took turns resting and rowing, parched lips and growling stomachs echoed in the night. In the distance the translator pointed at three fins circling the top of the ocean. "Sharks," he said.

Deathly still, Brian asked, "What do we do?"

"We'll try to row around them. It'll detour us slightly, but avoiding them might save our lives. Pray it doesn't throw us too off course and that they won't smell us, which will be a miracle in itself."

Brian silently prayed, "Lord, we don't want to be fish bait. You are the author and finisher of our fates. Keep those devourers distracted and away from us. Thank you."

Softly rowing miles away from the sharks and circling back around, they made it away from the fish frenzied creatures. After all the excitement and physical demands of the day, their bodies could no longer resist sleep. Exhaustion and dehydration began to take over. Soon speaking no longer became an option because of their parched, swollen, and cracking lips. They drifted off.

The waves rocked the boat high into the air. It came crashing down; water pouring in and rushing over the two men. Brian jumped to his feet almost capsizing them. The celestial body no longer showed its distant face above them, no longer offered help of guiding light. The translator reached his hand inside the soaked sleeping bag.

Brian looked awestruck. "My compass, I thought it was lost when the men took our packs?"

"No, I took a few things from your bag when you were asleep and placed them here. I couldn't tell you until now."

"Are we on the right course?" Brian's voice wavered. He knew the signs. He took his friends arm, "We're running out of time." Fear crept in like slime from a horror movie. He felt paralyzed.

"God will help us! Row now." The translator used his cupped hands to send the rising water back to its home.

Brian's taut muscles burned like a wildfire out of control. His forearm felt it like it would explode, but he did not stop. The morning light began to fight its way through the layers of cloud formations as if to say, "I see you. I'm here. This storm hasn't won yet." Then one of his tendons popped, and he screamed in agony, "I can't do it anymore!"

The translator took the oar from Brian's hand. He had to pry his fingers off because they had locked. "I'm sorry, my friend. I've failed you," the man conveyed his sorrow.

"No, no you haven't." Brian took his hand and prayed.

"Listen. Stop. Listen," his friend urged. A ship's horn could be lightly heard.

"We've nothing to signal them; in this fog they'll plow over us."

"Give me your shirt!" the translator yelled with enthusiasm.

"What?"

"Your shirt!"

Brian took off his white T-shirt. The translator stood and waved it as high as he could in the air. They yelled with all their waning strength and breath left in their lungs. The ship eased away from them. "No, Jesus, No! Please! Anything else in that sleeping bag!" Brian yelled above the now torrent waves.

The translator quickly unrolled and unzipped the bag. Brian's note pads and phone fell into the bottom of the wet boat. He quickly snatched the cell. "It has a flash light. I know an emergency code. If only it has power." He turned it on and flicked the switch. "Thank you, Jesus!" He said elated. In the barely lit darkness of the storm, it reflected out over the tossing waves. After a few minutes, two horns sounded from the ship.

"They've seen us!" He jumped up and down, tilting the boat and plummeting them both into the frigid water.

Brian came up gasping for air in time to see a huge wave roll over the top of his friend and take him under. "No!" he screamed and dove beneath the depths. It was impossible to see in the water. The searing pain in his arm left it practically useless, but Brian's prior swimming experience helped him use his legs and good arm to search for his friend.

The translator's head bobbed up like a bobber on a fishing line. Brian swam toward him as another wave catapulted him toward the ocean floor. He grabbed at his leg and yanked him upward. He kicked violently to the surface, pulling his friend with him. As the ships mighty engine drove toward them, Brian feared they would be swept under its great propeller's currents. Something crashed in on his head, dazing him for a moment. Realizing it to be a buoy, he clutched it and put it over his friend's head and under his arms, then yanked the rope as hard as he could.

The mariners pulled him up the side of the great craft. Brian could no longer keep afloat. His energy expended, he slipped underneath, feeling the icy grip of death suffocating the breath out of him. His life flashed before him and he sank deep into the aqueous grave. A seaman dove into the water and pulled Brian to safety with the help of his crew. When he awoke, water poured from every opening in his body, and he vomited violently. He felt a poke, great tightness in his chest, and then relief as the IV made its way into his bloodstream, supplying it with needed minerals and glucose. The translator stood above him, a blanket wrapped around his shoulders, and a grin as wide as the Saguaro River. "Thank you, you saved my life again."

"We never leave our partners. Thank you!" Brian said.

The doctor aboard the naval ship put a sling on his arm and hydrated them both well. The boat and all its contents sank to the ocean floor, but Brian sensed a peace and thankfulness to be alive. The pain medicine knocked him out, but as soon as he awoke, he asked if there was a way to send a message to his wife to let her know he was safe. The captain agreed to send the code to Maria as they made their way back to the mainland.

$$\infty$$

Maria sat on her Mom's deck watching Angel play in the sand box. Barbie lay on the beach chair in the sun sucking in the vitamin D as her doctor prescribed, "Fifteen minutes a day, no more." Eula came out with iced lemonade for everyone. Her sweet Mangosteen trees were some of the best in the neighborhood, and it brought her joy in sharing them often with others.

"Have you heard from him?" Eula asked as she looked at her daughter's forlorn face.

Maria hung her head, "No, I'm worried sick. I can barely eat. I make myself because of Angel. It's been over two weeks."

"I'm sorry, honey. I know he's coming home. I can feel it," her mom comforted.

Maria's ringtone played, "You are my sunshine." "I gotta take this mom, watch Angel, please." Like a teenager waiting on a call from her first love, she bounded down the steps to the side of the house to have privacy. "Brian, are you there? Brian?" The line went fuzzy and lost connection. Then a message came through a weird number. It read SS68-Captain-message from Brian. My dearly beloved, I am safe. Talk to you when I get inland. Love you to the moon and back.

Maria fell to her knees in the soft grass and cried, "Thank God! Thank you, God!" Tears poured from her eyes, cascading down her face. Eula came around the corner and picked her up to her feet, hugging her tightly and holding her up.

Angel came running up to them, "Mommy, are you okay?" the concerned little voice asked.

"I'm wonderful, Sweetheart. Daddy is coming home." She twirled her in the air.

"I hope this is the last trip for the year," Eula voiced.

"Oh, Mom, me too! No offense, but I'm ready to go home!" Maria exclaimed.

"Me too, Mommy!" Angel emphatically declared.

Chapter Twelve
No Place Like Home

Maria sat on the edge of the bed, yearning for the phone to ring. It had been three days since she received the encrypted message from the Captain. She managed to keep busy with washing and packing up her things for their return trip home.

Her distracted mind would wander off, imagining how Brian was really doing and the adventures he must have faced on the remote island. She would think of the pirates from the movies they had previously watched together and the dangers that lurked around every corner. Her heart knew it was silly, but the emotions would get the better of her every time.

She went to the kitchen, placed a bag of buttery Orville Redenbacher popcorn in the microwave, poured a glass of sweet tea, fluffed up her pillows, and placed *Pirates of the Caribbean* in the DVD player. It was one of their favorites. As the skeleton pirates were fighting, and the madam was screaming, the phone rang, and Maria nearly jumped out of her skin. She took a breath and pushed pause on the remote.

"Hello. Honey, is that you?" Maria asked.

"Yes," Brian's voiced cracked.

"Where are you?" she questioned.

"I'm, oh never mind. The important thing is I'm safe. How are you and my princess?"

No sooner than he asked the question, she came running into the room and jumped up beside Maria. Her mom put the phone on speaker.

"Hi, Princess. I miss you!" Brian said.

"Daddy," Angel screamed, "Daddy! Daddy, come home!"

"Yes, Sweetie, calm down. I know you're excited. I'll be home soon. I don't have much time. I love you. Give mommy a hug for me. I miss you, but I'll see you soon."

Angel did a roll on the bed in her delight. "Tata!" she exclaimed.

"Excellent! Now sit here." She tucked Angel in beside her and turned her attention to Brian. "Good, 'cause there's been a lot going on here. We miss you. We need you," Maria conveyed.

"I know. I miss you too. I should be home within the next week. I'll call you. Listen, I gotta go. I love you both!" Brian hung up.

Maria could hear a lot of noise in the background, but couldn't make out what was being said. She prayed he would remain safe and get home to them quickly. She called her mom and dad at Larry's house. They were having supper together. "Mom, can you put me on speaker phone, please?"

"Yes, go ahead?" Eula responded.

"Brian is coming home within the next week," Maria cried.

Whoops and hollers echoed through the room, all expressing their sincere gratitude for his safety and return home.

"Mom, I need to go home. Would you be able to go with Barbie to her last two treatments and take care of her? I need to get the house cleaned and ready."

"Sure, I think so. Let me grab my planner from my purse. There are a couple of things, but I can reschedule them. I hope you'll meet us to eat or something when you pick him up from the airport?"

"We'll try. Thanks, Mom. Will you be home soon? Barbie and Angel are asleep. My mind is racing, and I would like to go pick up a few supplies before I go to bed."

"Yes, we should be home within the hour."

∞

Brian could not believe all the hoopla he had to go through to clear the ship and prove his identity. Even though the captain supported him, the commander of the port spied him suspiciously. The translator questioned exhaustively, finally threw his hands up in disgust and murmured something in his foreign tongue. He used the captain's phone and quickly conveyed an urgent request to his boss inland. After hours, a long, black limousine arrived, and a distinguished gentleman stepped out with briefcase in hand. He marched up to the commander's post and handed him copies of both men's passports.

Frustrated, the commander called for the passengers. "You are free to go, but don't expect our men to rescue you from these water's again!"

Brian and the translator scurried off the boat. All they wanted for the moment was a hot shower and real food. With his injuries, he barely managed to get toast down during the tossing voyage back. The driver took them to the hotel where their remaining belongings were stored.

"Thank you!" the translator said as he shook the driver's hand.

"Who is that really? I've observed your responses this trip, and you're never friendly to a stranger."

The man laughed, "He is my brother!" he exclaimed.

The men parted ways to their rooms, but agreed to meet for supper later in the evening. Brian showered a long time, allowing the hot water to pour over him and soothe his weary soul. His thoughts were full of all he had lost and gained, the life and death situations, and seeds planted. He thanked God for sparing him time and again. He would be forever grateful to this new friend he called translator. His arm injuries would be a bittersweet reminder of the cost of this trip. It would take a few months of physical therapy and possibly surgery to get it back to full capacity. Even after showering, he looked rugged, tattered and worn. The sun's damage to his skin, the cuts and bruises up and down his arms and legs, the teeth marks on his hand from the viper's bite, all signs of an adventure well fought. The tiger fangs that hung around his neck were a true symbol of the brotherhood formed. How it managed to stay on during the battle with the waves was beyond Brian. Miracles happen every day, and he had never been more convinced of this than now.

∞

Angel ran to her daddy, arms held high. He scooped her up into his embrace with his one good arm. Brian's laughter and smile warmed Maria's heart and made her insides dance. She stood with her hands clasped over her mouth as he made his way to her. He looked gaunt, dark circles hung under his eyes, hair disheveled, and his right arm hung in a sling. The fingers sticking out from his bandage appeared to be discolored. His appearance was far from what she expected.

"You're home!" she said embracing him a little too tight.

"Ouch!" he groaned.

"I'm sorry. Are you okay? You look tired and beat up. What happened to your arm?" Maria asked. She was worried about him and her furrowed brow showed it.

He squeezed her. "I'm good. I'm home with you. I've much to tell you, but not now." He nodded at Angel.

Maria drove from the airport toward her parents' home. Angel sang her ABC's loudly in the backseat, begging for his attention. He reached back and gave her a high five and handed her some goldfish from his bag.

"Why don't you rest, honey? We'll have plenty of time to share," Maria encouraged.

"Okay, I'll try. Brian starred out at the night sky. The stars hidden behind the city lights were nothing like the celestial bodies and the entourage of stars exuding light in the glorious sky of Neotarama. He drifted off to sleep.

Twenty-five minutes later, Maria gently shook his shoulder. "Honey, we're here."

As he walked in the door of Eula and Aaron's home, he was reminded once again of how much he is loved as they showered him with hugs. A huge banner hung on the doorposts reading, "Welcome Home." The smell of freshly baked bread and cookies filled the house. Fine china and a glass baking dish housing Maria's homemade lasagna set the dinner table.

Nothing had ever tasted as good as that meal surrounded by the people he cherished the most. Brian told them the story of the island, at least what he felt at liberty to share. He showed them the fang marks from the snake. They gasped, oooed and awed.

"It sounds like a tall tale to me!" Larry razzed him, but deep inside he worried at the way Brian looked. "I'm kidding."

Words could not begin to express Brian's thankfulness to be home with his family and back to work at the hospital. He did not understand the dreams haunting him. Though he experienced a lot of trauma during his most recent trip, he felt there was more significance to the scenes playing before him when he slept at night. Often he woke in a cold sweat and breathless, many images of the black beast chasing him ran through the pages of his mind. The people of Neatorama, their loyalty, and the message given to the chief all left its mark heavy in his heart.

Desperate for some answers to the plaguing meaning of his nightmares, Brian searched the internet for analogies and metaphors representing darkness, battle, and death. One evening in a determined frenzy he came upon the meaning of the name Neatorama. It meant to dig out or bring something to light. He sat staring at his computer screen in amazement. Maria came up behind him almost startling him. "Honey, don't do that. I could've swung around and hit you," he said sharply.

"I'm sorry. Are you okay? Babe, you've got to get some rest. I'm worried about you. You weren't home a week before you went back to work. The physical therapy and pain are draining enough. You need your rest to heal properly. Remember the doctor said if it doesn't heal properly within the next few weeks, you'll need surgery. You've been up and down every night. What are you looking at?"

"I know. If only I had some answers to these dreams. Look what I found, the name of the island" He pointed to the screen. "Wow, I've been looking at it for an hour, pretty astounding, huh?"

"Yes, it is. Please, come to bed," she pleaded.

"Okay, I will I promise." He pulled her into his lap, and she snuggled up to his chest.

"I've missed you! I wish you could be home for a week or so. We need to catch up."

"Now you know I can't take more time off. I'll see if I can get off early one night this week, and we'll go out for some date time, okay?"

She got up and swayed to the door, purposefully teasing him to come back to bed.

Brian played with the idea of seeing one of the psychologists at work that specialized in dreams, but he did not know where the man stood spiritually, and it could be a problem if they had differing views. "He'll either believe and help me, or lock me in the mental ward," he told Maria one night at supper.

"Shouldn't you talk to Pastor Stroke or my dad first? The Bible says among counselors there is safety," she advised.

"You worry too much. He's a dream doctor and a professional. Look, it'll be okay. Now to change the subject, how's Barbie doing?"

"She's better, but I don't understand if this treatment is doing what it's supposed to. Why is she still going between doing really well and then lousy?"

"From a doctor's standpoint, I'd say the medications work in each patient differently. But as a friend, I say she seems depressed. Chronic illness wears on a patient; sometimes they need counseling to deal with it. Will she be up this weekend?"

"Yes, Mom said she'd ride up with her. She's enjoyed her staying with them, especially since we came home."

"Eula's gift is nurturing; she's everyone's mama, that's for sure. I'll talk to Barbie, okay?" Did you hear anything from the adoption agency while I was away?"

"Thanks. No, but I've not time to pursue it either. I took Angel out of dance lessons here after the recital and put her in by Mom's for the last session. She did well at her performance. You'd have been so proud. I recorded it for you. We can watch now if you like?"

"Sure, honey. I'd like too. Have I told you how much I love you lately?" He snuggled close to her ear. "I love you more than all the water in all the oceans in the world!"

Brian sat watching in awe as Angel danced across the stage in her purple ballerina costume with a beaded tiara on her little head. "Could she look any more like a princess than she does at this moment?" His heart filled with joy sprinkled with a little sadness.

∞

Waves, tossing, turning, going under, deeper and intense darkness. Brian woke up gasping for air. Throwing the covers off, he headed for the bathroom and threw water on his face.

"Honey, are you okay?" Maria asked.

"Yes, I'm sorry for waking you. Go back to sleep, please. I'm going to sit in my recliner and pray."

Her words from the previous conversation about getting godly counsel reverberated in his mind. He decided to pick up his Bible. It felt good to thumb through the pages. He missed these quiet moments to study and contemplate the deeper meanings of the ageless text.

He lay back in his recliner, turned the pages to the concordance in the back of his Scofield Study Bible, and looked up the word, "counselors." He then turned to Proverbs 11:14, "Where there is no counsel the people fall; but in the multitude of counselors there is safety."

He loved this Scripture. It did confirm what Maria emphasized to him. Brian drifted off to sleep with the Bible in his lap.

Angel woke up in the night, climbed out of her bed and made her way into the kitchen. She tugged at the refrigerator door knocking a ceramic fish magnet to the floor. It shattered in three pieces. Brian hurdled out of his chair, nearly knocking over the table lamp, sending his Bible through the air. He rushed into the kitchen eyes wide with fear. He grabbed the broom from the open hall closet and held it tight in his hand. He could not see the little form behind the kitchen bar. He lunged around the counter without thinking, fight mechanism took over, and he barely missed the child's head with the handle. Angel dropped her milk and ran crying to her mom in great sobs of grief, "Mommy! Mommy! Mommy!"

Maria was jarred out of a deep sleep, gathered her daughter into her arms, and sang "Jesus Loves Me" to calm her. The child's body shook uncontrollably. Brian set foot in the master bedroom cautiously. He stood in shock not understanding what ensued, although he knew the full ramifications of what could have happened if he had hit Angel in the head with the makeshift weapon.

He fell to his knees beside the bed in front of them. "I'm sorry, Sweetie. You startled Daddy. I would never hurt you." Brian placed his head in his hands.

The tears in her daddy's eyes softened Angel's spirit. She broke free from Maria's embrace, threw her arms around her daddy's neck, and gently said, "It's okay, Daddy, don't cry."

He pulled her into his arms and stroked her brow, kissing her forehead, "Do you want to sleep with us tonight?" She shook her head yes and curdled back into the bed with Maria. Brian climbed in behind his wife and whispered, "I'll explain in the morning. I'm pretty shaken."

He had not told them all that occurred on the island. His weary soul began to realize the beast was slowly creeping into the present, with fear taunting him daily. After a thorough discussion with Maria the next morning, the decision was made for him to follow through with making an appointment to see the doctor at work. Maybe the trauma he experienced awakened more in him than he previously realized. The settling into routine felt good, but this would not be his new normal.

∞

"Man, it's good to be back," Larry commented.

"It's wonderful to have you back on the job," Aaron replied. "Did you hear the biopsy results yet?"

"No, I see the doctor for a follow-up in a week or so. Adaline keeps up with our calendar. I'm no good with that stuff. Did Brian call you? He wants to meet with us and Pastor Stroke. He needs some accountability and counsel, he said. From what he relayed, he sees me as his Timothy, you as his Barnabas, and Pastor Stroke as his Paul. I'd never heard it put in that particular fashion before." He chuckled.

"I have. We had an evangelist come to the church and taught on it one time. It hit home pretty good. As a man, it made me think of how important the brothers in the Body of Christ are to each other, how much we need one another. We all have an important part to play in the brotherhood. I can't remember the name of the evangelist, but he's first-rate. The DVD is at my house if you'd like to borrow it sometime."

"Okay, thanks. Adaline and I've got something we want to talk to them about; maybe we could do a picnic while the weather is still nice out. The Veterans Park in Anthem Way would be good. Would Friday work for y'all?"

"I think so. I'll check with Eula and confirm."

"Great! I'll call Stroke and Brian to see if it fits their schedule. If not, maybe Saturday?"

"No, Saturday we've the Huskey job to finish up, and I think this weekend Brian may be on call. Keep me posted. I got to go check on this other job site. Glad you're doing well. See you later." Aaron waved bye.

Everyone's schedules were all over the place; Maria needed to take Barbie for a follow-up appointment in Phoenix on Friday morning. It worked perfect for Brian, because he was off before a long weekend on call. The group decided to meet late afternoon at the park Larry suggested.

A railroad track dotted the scenery around Anthem Way's Veteran's park. The memorial stood tall and proud, commemorating the lives of those who gave to provide for the freedoms enjoyed today. The playground and water pad bustled with lively children playing tag and trying to catch the water shooting up from the holes. One little girl sat obstinate on a hole, refusing to budge or share her treasured spot.

The large red, blue, and yellow canopy jungle gym offered fun for every age. Park benches stretched out at different spots throughout the area under shade trees and near the water, giving a quiet respite from the bustle of busy city life. The waterfalls were a soothing reprieve of solitude in the mind and made great backdrops for pictures. Gazebos and picnic tables allowed families and friends the gift of time together. Whether celebrating, contemplating, or enjoying company, Brian felt

Larry picked the perfect place. Nearby fast food establishments and the all-around beauty of the area provided a great family picnic.

The geese and ducks scattered about the lake like springs of grass. The geese's elongated midnight necks, heads held high and their cheeks caressed by touches of snow continued their proud squawking to let their presence be known.

After blessings and supper, the ladies talked together under the shade of the colorful umbrellas, while Angel frolicked on the playground donning her princess tiara and cap Mema made her. She begged Maria to climb up and slide with her. "Not today, honey; mommy's leg hurts. Remember I burnt it yesterday doing the yard."

"Mema will." Her grandmother followed her around and chased her down the bridge, up the slide, and sat Angel on her lap to coast down the curvy obstacle. They climbed over pretend rocks. Eula refused to crawl on her knees, but she could practically do all the other activities required by her persistent grandchild. She did not want to be one who sat on the sidelines. Her heart treasured these moments, knowing how soon they would disappear and the child would be grown. She peered over at Maria from behind the rock wall where she hid from Angel as they played hide and seek. Sweet, fond memories of her as a little girl flooded Eula's soul.

The men sat at the picnic table on the other end of the long lake under the native shade trees, admiring the variety of cacti complementing the park's scenery along the rocks' decorative edge. Larry and Aaron brainstormed ideas for their flourishing landscaping business.

Brian brought their time to order and shared with them about the nightmares, the near collision with Angel, and the fear trying to strangle him. He told them a lot about his journey, things he kept private up to this point and about seeing the doctor at work. It scared him to think he might actually be suffering from minor PTSD associated with the trauma from the island and the fear of not making it home to his family. It was imperative he dealt with his emotions quickly and needed a good support group to keep him on track with his healing goals. He felt these things would help keep him focused and from doing anything irrational because of his fears.

He received good counsel and different perspectives from each of the three men. They all agreed to keep him accountable by calling or texting him weekly and praying for him daily. He agreed when they called he could not use the excuse he was too busy to deal with any issues they saw arising. He confessed up front that in the past he had used this to justify when he did not want to handle a situation. "It's getting dark. Maybe we should head back to the ladies?" Brian suggested.

Larry grabbed his arm. "There's something Adaline and I need to talk to you and Maria about. Can Aaron and Eula or Barbie take Angel?

Aaron sensed urgency in Larry's tone and piped up, "Yes, we can. I'll walk over and send the women your way."

"No, Adaline isn't too comfortable these days. She isn't going to walk over here again. Maybe we can go to the coffee shop I saw on the way in, across from Taco Bell and McDonalds?" he stated.

The grandparents gathered the precious toddler. Barbie agreed to ride back with them too. Pastor Stroke said his goodbyes and headed out.

"Meet y'all at the house," Barbie said.

"Bye-bye." Angel blew Brian and Maria a kiss. "See you later, alligator!" she yelled.

"After while, crocodile," her mommy responded.

The four met at the coffee shop a couple blocks away from the park. "What would you like? My treat." Brian asked.

Everyone rattled off their orders; Adaline and Maria headed to the bathroom, and the guys took four comfy plush seats in the corner. "What's the imminence?"

"It's not an emergency; we've something important to talk to you about. We're excited, that's all. Here come the ladies. Be patient." Larry turned his attention to his wife. "Decaf, hazelnut latte like you like it and pumpkin loaf since Brian's treating. Baby's needs a pick-me-up too. I'm sure he's hungry by now." He chuckled.

"Very funny, but yummy, thanks. This is nice, having time with just the four of us. We haven't in such a long time. Soon we'll be all tied up changing diapers and taking care of our baby. Speaking of him, Larry are you ready to share why we wanted this special alone time with them?" Adaline asked.

"Yes, yes I would, but first a toast to best friends for life. Thanks for always standing by my side through thick and thin."

They raised their cups and tapped them together. Brian raised his left eyebrow. The way he did anytime he felt Larry coming up with a scheme. He knew it would cost him something or get him in trouble. "This sounds like a con job to me."

"Now, I'm hurt you would think such a thing, albeit probably warranted after some of the shenanigans I've put you through over the years," Larry retorted and lowered his head in a childish pouting fashion.

"Oh, come on. I'm kidding. Tell us what's going on. Look at Maria. She's sitting on the edge of her chair already. Curiosity killed a cat, but satisfaction brought it back," Brian teased.

Maria cackled and snorted, and then they all burst out laughing.

After a few minutes Brian interrupted them, "Seriously now."

"Adaline and I would like you to be Joshua Aaron's godparents. We'd like to draw up legal documents saying such. If anything happens to the both of us, we want you to adopt our son and raise him as your own." Larry and his wife held hands, faces beaming brightly.

The glow on Adaline's face and look of assurance in her eyes was irresistible. Maria did not even think about her next words; they were automatic. "Of course we will."

"Maria, may I speak to you outside a minute." Brain motioned her over to the door.

"I'm sorry, I guess I should make sure you feel the same way, but here we're trying to adopt another child. It makes sense to me; we would agree to do this for your lifelong friend in the event, God forbid, it did happen. They'd do it in a minute for us." She smiled sweetly.

"Okay, maybe you're right. It does mean being there to help whether something happens or not, keeping them accountable as parents too." Brian countered.

"Babe, you've being keeping Larry answerable for as long as I can remember."

"True." He pulled her into his arms. "How did you become this wise?"

"Being married to you, I guess." She laughed and kissed him.

They walked back in and sat down. "If you need time to think about it, we understand. It's a big responsibility raising someone else's child." Adaline covered her mouth. "I'm sorry; you know that better than anyone I guess." She said shyly.

"We don't need time to think about it. We'd be delighted to be your son's godparents. Keeping you on track as a father and husband would be an honor. God forbid anything happening to either of you, but if the incidence occurs, we would adopt your baby. However, I do need to ask a question. Adaline it might be hard for you, but what about your parents? Would they fight to have your child?" Brian questioned.

"My parents don't hold the same values as we do. We aren't even speaking since the wedding. It's their choice, not mine. I doubt they would want the child of a man they abhor. Sorry, honey." She squeezed Larry's leg. "I don't want my parents raising my son. They were distant when I was growing up, working constantly; someone else always took care of me. Financial support is not the only thing a child needs. I want him to be loved and cared for in a deeper way than I ever was." She began to cry.

Maria moved over and put her arm around Adaline. "We are in unity. Let's pray. As long as we all have peace about it, consider it done."

Brian prayed. They waited a few minutes in silence giving the Holy Spirit time to speak to them.

"Thank you. You are the most balanced and loving people we know. I realize you're not perfect, but we aspire to be the parents you are." Adaline remarked. They hugged Brian and Maria.

"Thank you; I wouldn't want it to be anyone else," Larry said.

Chapter Thirteen
TAKING A STAND

The tall, distinguished glass building lined in silver trim stood out as the backdrop for the other smaller modern buildings. Larry never liked this type of architecture. It reminded him of the swaying buildings and earthquakes he experienced in his early childhood years in California. The parking garage was packed with cars like sardines in a can. He could not imagine how the narrow parking spaces could be safe. The heavy doors entering the main floor led to the surgeon's elaborate office on the first floor.

The receptionist asked for Larry's insurance card and driver's license. She handed him a clip-board with seven papers to fill out and sign. "Am I buying a house?" he said jokingly.

Without batting an eye or smiling, not changing her demeanor at all, she handed him a pen and asked him to be seated.

"Well, they must have hired her for her ability, definitely not for charm. Wow! I don't like filing out all this paperwork. Half of my history died with my parents, the other with my grandparents." Larry began to fidget and became increasingly agitated.

Adaline tried to calm him, "If you don't know put 'N/A.' It's okay."

"Larry," the nurse called. He handed the clipboard to the lady behind the desk. "Step on the scale, please." She led them to a sitting area. "The lab technician will be with you shortly. He'll take your vitals as well as your labs. When he is finished, please make your way to exam room three. The doctor will be in soon."

They did as instructed. The surgeon came in and tested Larry's reflexes, coordination, and eyes. He asked several questions. "I'm impressed at how well you are doing. Are you back to work?"

"Yes," Larry answered.

"Any dizziness or cognitive problems?" he asked.

"No, I feel great!" Larry exclaimed.

"The biopsy results were negative; the tumor is benign as I predicted. However, benign or cancerous brain tumors can be dangerous. They are extremely erratic and often grow at accelerated rates. The chance of another mass forming at some point is high. We would like to prevent that through chemotherapy. It'll kill any remaining unhealthy cells and keep them from spreading to other parts of the brain. Did you follow-up with the oncologist?"

"No, I've no desire to take chemo. I appreciate all you've done, but as you said, it is benign." Larry stood up to shake his hand.

The doctor continued on the path of conversation he was taking, "If you're concerned about the chemo, let me explain. It comes in a pill taken once a day. Most patients have little if any side effects. You go about normal life. It's not a big deal."

"I must disagree. I may not know a lot, but I do know chemotherapy kills healthy cells, along with the unhealthy. The people I've known who had it, experienced major side effects or took several medications to prevent them. It's no big deal to you! You're not taking it!" Larry grabbed Adaline's hand and stormed out of the room.

"Can you believe that arrogant..." He let his words trail off. "Sorry. The old me coming out," Larry apologized.

"He's only repeating what he's been taught in the medical community. They do what they see every other doctor doing and some have great success," Adaline conveyed.

Larry opened the door for her and shut it firmly when she secured her seatbelt.

"They don't make these harnesses for pregnant women. Breathe, honey. Talk to Brian and get his medical opinion. Speak with Aaron about what they've done," she encouraged.

"We've a baby coming. I don't like someone speaking something on me like it's a definite thing going to happen. It angers me, because it feels like they play on people's fears. Most doctors I've known act like you don't know anything." Larry swerved to keep from hitting another car as he pulled out from the stop sign. He looked up to heaven and said, "Okay, I got it. I'll calm down."

"It's true, but you don't have to do anything you don't want to do. Right now, I'm starving. May we go for Chinese?" Adaline asked.

Larry had to laugh. No matter the mood, situation, or emotion, hunger always came to the forefront for Adaline lately.

As they walked into the restaurant, Adaline spotted Aaron and Eula sitting in a corner booth. "Fancy meeting you here. Want to join us?" Aaron said.

"It might be a tight squeeze," Adaline acknowledged her ever-growing belly that hung a little past her pink and black striped maternity top.

"Okay, we can move over there." Eula pointed to a six chair table.

"It's definitely no accident meeting you here today. Let us get our plates before my wife falls on the floor from starvation, and we'll tell you all about it." Larry winked at Adaline.

"Funny, a minute ago you were a raging bull, not you're a comedian," Adaline retorted.

Larry filled them in on the doctor's report and his feelings about it. Aaron understood the fears and frustrations associated with it, but also told him not to be so hard on all doctors. After all, his best friend fell into that category.

Eula shared with Adaline and Larry the importance of a healthy diet and juicing. She said she would be willing to help them make some changes if they wanted.

"You would need to be willing to get rid of the soda though. I know it won't be easy, but you can do it. Maybe after the baby shower we can talk more about it since you'll be at our house anyway," she sympathetically expressed.

"Mom, I'll have to think on that," Larry replied.

They turned to lighter conversation. Eula knew when to let it go; she learned the hard way not to push the matter. Good friends walked away from their relationship when they learned the value of good eating, getting rid of dairy and sugar, and how it affected the body. They were eager to share their lifestyle changes with all they loved because it influenced their lives radically. Eula and Aaron wanted others to reap from the benefits of healthy living, but often people could only see the sacrifices, although the assets far outweighed them.

Chapter Fourteen
Precious Memories

Barbie felt much better after her last treatment at Mayo. Her strength seemed to be returning and she had fewer bad days and more good ones. Stress played a huge part in regulating how she felt. Aaron and Eula did not push her at all about moving out. They made her feel welcomed and encouraged her to do what she could. Letting go of the job she loved a few months prior pained her, but the doctor recommended she file the paperwork for short-term disability, and his staff helped her do so. She consoled herself in the fact it was only temporary, and her body would heal quicker with proper rest and less anxiety. Her work on English literature had taken off through a blog she created.

It made her feel alive and brought back fond memories of her mother. Pastor Stroke taught her how to release the negative emotions related to her mom's death and glean from the positive heritage from her mom. Volunteering at the library gave her an outlet too, and it delighted her to be helping others investigate what books or genre they might enjoy.

Maria and Eula asked her to make the cake for Adaline's baby shower. She loved to bake and found a precious lamb made of fondant to decorate the top. She felt honored at such a request. The icing would be made of whipped cream, as it was Adaline's favorite. Barbie found just the right tint of blue, and white dots would ornament the sides.

They all pitched in to buy her the stroller and matching infant car seat she wanted from Target. Brian insisted Maria buy her the matching port-a-crib. She teased him endlessly, saying he was becoming an old softy and getting as bad as the ladies at buying for the babies.

The shower blessed Adaline to tears. The ladies of the congregation spoiled her immensely with hand-quilted blankets, baby clothes, diapers, and necessities. Her sister Rose showered her with things for her, a spa day, hand and foot kit, and gift cards to all her favorite stores and restaurants. Each of the women in attendance wrote a blessing or Scripture for her to reflect on in the weeks and months to come, little notes of encouragement, and reminders of God's faithfulness and love.

The men were invited to the last half for cake, pictures, and group prayer over Larry, Adaline, and their soon-to-be-born son, Joshua Aaron. Adaline had a special engraved cherry mahogany wood plaque made with Aaron's name encircling her son's and the meaning of both, Exalted, Bold and Generous. "You've been a great example of Jesus' love and life; therefore, our son will bear your name." Larry honored Aaron with the special gift.

Extremely humbled by this expression of love, Aaron pulled them into his embrace with a great bear hug.

Maria stepped away at the end to retrieve Angel from Rose's daughter who watched her in the play room. This touched her to the core, bringing up her own memories of her son, Isaiah, and she wanted nothing more than to embrace her little girl. She held her squirming child and showered her with kisses.

"Mommy, butterflies." Maria touched her long eye lashes to Angel's soft cheek. "Now Eskimo." They rubbed noses together. How could she be sad with such a priceless gift in her arms?

"Mommy, loves you so very much!" Angel wrapped her petite arms around Maria's shoulders and hugged her back, patting her like Maria used to do when she was a baby.

After helping Eula and Aaron clean up, Brian and Maria decided to head back home, even though it was getting late. He did not need to be at the hospital until 10 am, but they did not want to rush back in the morning, knowing that Angel would sleep all the way.

"Are you sure you don't want to stay?" Eula pleaded.

"Mom, don't worry. We'll be fine. I've made this trip a million times. I could do it blind-folded." Brian teased.

"The elk come out at night; the deer too. I just don't like it," Eula protested.

"Come on honey, we'll pray for them. We men think of it as an adventure. When we were young, we did it all the time, remember?" Aaron comforted.

"Reminder, we hit a doe in the dark. What a mess!" Eula reminded him.

They circled up and prayed. Adaline and Larry left an hour before to unload packages and sort stuff in the nursery. She already experienced some Braxton hicks contractions and needed to rest with her legs up.

"Call me when you get home. You know I won't sleep until I know you are safe," Eula said as she waved good-bye from the front yard.

"We love you to the moon and back!" Maria yelled out her window.

Angel also chimed in, "I love you too!" and blew kisses with her hands.

"Since Bergie's is closed, do you want me to go through the drive through at Dutch Brothers and get us a drink?" he asked Maria

"Coconut milk with a splash of hazelnut please," Angel said.

They could not help but laugh. She definitely knew what she wanted.

"Sure, that would be nice." Maria played lightly on his arm with her fingers. Her heart resonated with gratitude. She could have lost him on the island. Goose bumps rose underneath the hair on his forearm in response to her touch. "Will there always be a scar on your hand?"

"Probably, but I don't mind if you don't." He looked sincerely into her eyes, but quickly brought his attention back to the road. "I sure miss mom and dad's old brown Buick Regal. It had the full front seat. In that car you could've slid right over here beside me, nice and cozy."

"Sweet, you were too young to take advantage of that perk." She giggled. "Wow, this is the quietest I've seen a DB drive-up. Are they closed?" Maria questioned.

No sooner had the words played out of his mouth, a young man stuck his head out the window and signaled for them to move forward.

"Good evening. What can I get you?"

"I'll have a blended Caramelizer, a coconut milk chai, and the young lady in the back will place her order." Brian smiled wide and pushed Angel's window release.

"I want a coconut milk with a splash of hazelnut, please." Angel's dimples and contagious smile flashed to the man.

"What a cutie! Your drink is on me," he responded and turned to Brian. "What are you up to tonight?"

Curious about the conversation flow, Maria answered, "Going home from a baby shower."

"Nice, I love children. I had a lot of siblings. Here's your drinks."

"Well, thank you. Maybe your calling is children's ministry." Brian took their drinks and gave the spiked haired, polite, twentyish year old a good tip.

"Thanks. Something to think about, I'm finishing my degree in Philosophy at ASU."

"Nice, stick to your dreams. God has a plan for your life. We'll pray He directs you to the best path for you. Hold on a second."

"Maria, I can't open my door. Can you grab a study and book from the back?"

She got out and returned with the requested items.

"Thanks." He turned his attention back to the young man. "I would like to give you these as a gift. The Bible says if you seek with all of your heart, you'll find the answers you're looking for. Ask Jesus to make it real to you."

"I don't know. Philosophy does talk about keeping an open mind." He rubbed his chin. "I'll do it."

A car pulled up behind them. "Blessings to you," Brian and Maria said simultaneously.

"I'm glad we decided to stop. I don't think that conversation was an accident or a coincidence," Brian said.

Angel fell asleep with the kid's cup in her hand and straw in her mouth. Maria adjusted the rear view mirror in a way Brian could see her.

"Adorable! She's growing fast. Her words have improved and she's making full sentences. I'm proud of the work you've done with her." He complemented his wife.

"Thanks. I don't want you to go again. I know you didn't get all the answers you wanted, but it's too dangerous, and we need you. Your arm is on the mends. I'm happy for that, but the pain it has caused you physically, emotionally, and the risk of losing you isn't worth it," She spoke firmly and adamantly.

"I know. I've been thinking about it a lot. I don't even know what the future holds for my grants. Every year it is different. The staff and students I've been working with at Northern Arizona University have been experimenting with the items I brought back from Neatorama, but we've a long way to go. It could be years before any real benefit comes from that particular research. Thanks for your patience with me. I promise you this; I won't go unless we both agree. I love you to the moon and back." He reached for her hand and pressed it up to his lips.

"I love you too," Maria whispered.

She turned the radio knob to 90.3 and laid her head on the pillow against the window. It wasn't long before she drifted off to sleep.

In the darkness Brian prayed for the man at the coffee shop and his family. He longed to be healed of the night terrors haunting him. The psychologist at work said it could take months or even years to overcome the trauma he experienced, but they were working through many of the fears of loss he had suffered through the years. The physical therapy had done wonders for his hand and arm, but the cold wrapped around the areas like a python around its prey and caused him a great deal of stiffness and pain.

His daydreaming took him back to the brave warriors he fought with. He could not keep from wondering how they were doing now. A sudden pop and thump as the tire rotated on the flat spot brought Brian back to the present. The red service engine light came on almost immediately. Smoke started spewing from the front of the car. He eased over onto the shoulder and at that moment his headlights lit upon four gigantic elk crossing the road. His mouth dropped opened, and he shook Maria. "Honey, look," he pointed to the front of the car.

"Can you believe those gorgeous creatures cause wrecks? Hey, where's the smoke coming from?" She voiced.

"I think we've got a busted radiator and a flat, but it may have saved our lives. I'll go check it out." He exited the car. "Pop the hood, please!" He yelled to Maria.

She crawled over to the driver's side and did as commanded. "Be careful. The steam can blind you. My dad singed his eyebrows one time from the same thing."

He peered inside. "I need the flashlight from the glove compartment."

She jumped out of the car, only to land in mud to her shins. "Oh hon, you didn't tell me."

He cackled. She glared. "Okay, it's not funny. I must be tired. Definitely the radiator." He walked around the driver's side and to the back. Flashing the light on his tires he responded, "Weird, it doesn't look flat, but I can't tell with all the red mire down there. I'll grab a gallon of water and towel from the trunk. We can at least wash the stuff off you."

"Brian, it's cold up here. I'm going to need to change. I'll climb in the back with Angel," Maria replied.

"You can't get in the car? Come here and let me do this. Then you can change. That should be fun."

She smacked his arm. "I'm glad you are finding this comical, mister. I get uptight over anything mechanical concerning vehicles."

"What?" He rinsed off her legs and shoes. Then helped her maneuver around Angel in the back seat and she changed.

"You could call road side assistance. The number is on the dash," Maria fussed.

"Good idea." He dialed the number and talked to a friendly person back east somewhere.

"It could take thirty minutes for a tow truck to get here. They will take us to the nearest shop, and we can call a cab to get home. In the morning the insurance company will arrange for a rental until our car is repaired. I guess we'll listen to mom the next time she tells us to stay overnight at their house. Maybe you should call her?" Brian requested.

"Thank God they're okay. It could've been much worse," Aaron said as he hung up the phone. Eula immediately dropped to her knees and he bent down beside her. "Thank you, Jesus, for protecting our children."

The cab driver made Brian nervous. He barely spoke a lick of English, but he managed to get them home. His piercing nut brown eyes glared into Brian.

"Thank you," Brian said as he tipped the driver. He told himself, "You're being paranoid because you're exhausted."

He ushered his family safely in doors, peeked out the blinds to make sure the driver drove off, and turned on their security system. Maria carried Angel up to her room, but Brian insisted she sleep with them for the night.

Brian barely slept, thinking of the look in the driver's eyes. It clung to him through the night. The man's skin had the same lustrous cocoa color as Angels' and his eyes almost black like hers too. Throughout the night he would get up to check the windows and doors. He would look out the front blinds for the bright yellow cab.

The next morning came with a throbbing headache and two Tylenol before Brian made his phone calls. He called the co-instructor presenting the class to inform her of their situation, and let her know he would not be able to help with the session. He asked her to reschedule or precede without him. The Chief of the hospital called to check on Brian and his family. He felt blessed by his concern and asked if he could take a personal day to deal with the pressing issues at hand. He reassured him that he would be back in his office by Tuesday morning.

Then Brian prayed about how to ask someone to stay with Angel and Maria while he worked for the next few days. He did not want to scare his wife, especially since the incidence could be coincidence and nothing at all. He was not comfortable leaving them alone. Somehow he needed to get a message to Rojomen that he believed they were in danger.

Larry called to check in on Brian and Maria the following day. He asked if they could come to Flagstaff for a few days and get out of the heat. Adaline felt miserable with the temperatures soaring. He confirmed the hours he would be working and let them know.

"Maria, honey, where are you?" He found her deep in her closet looking through a portfolio of pictures. "Oh sweetie, you sure it's a good idea to pull Isaiah's box down right now?"

"Why not? I miss him. Adaline's shower brought up a lot of emotions for me. I need to see him."

He held her. "I know. They called and asked to come up for a few days."

"Why? I love them, but it's not great timing."

"I know, but the insurance company is taking forever getting a rental. I need our vehicle for work. I would feel better if they were here, and they asked to come because of the heat. Plus, he sent the legal papers by priority mail, and we should get them today. He wants to go over them while they are here. I think we should celebrate being godparents, don't you?" He pulled her to himself, trying to lighten the tension between them. He played with the curls around her face and kissed her lightly on the forehead.

"You are too much!" Maria giggled.

Angel toddled in and yanked at her mama's pants leg. "I'm hungry, Mommy. Snack, please."

"Wow, I'm not sure that's good manners. Sounds like demanding with a please on the end." Brian scooped her up in his arms, looking into her chestnut eyes. "Maybe it's how we say it too. May I have a snack, please?" he said emphasizing softly with his tone. Angel repeated his words and rubbed her nose with the back of her hand.

Brian could see a small dot of blood on her finger. "Have you been picking your nose again?"

Angel hung her head and sadly said, "Yes."

"Does a princess pick her nose? Have you ever seen any of the little princesses on your cartoons do it?" Maria asked, handing her Puffs.

"If you do that, your nose will bleed and ruin your pretty dresses. We wouldn't want that, would we?" Brian asked.

Angel shook her head. "No, Daddy."

"I'll clean her up in the bathroom. Let's go wash your hands, and then we can have some of your mom's delicious scrambled eggs," Brian said loud enough for Maria to hear him.

Chapter Fifteen
ETERNITY'S THRESHOLD

Brian met Mrs. Kelly in the emergency room for her daughter. Missy's cancer fell into remission over six months ago. He became concerned she would be back in the ER for a falling episode.

"Missy, what're you doing here?" he said lightheartedly. "Were you missing me?"

"I fell down today and hurt my leg," the eleven year old replied.

"Did you feel dizzy?" Brian questioned as he examined her leg.

"No, but I did lose my balance. Doc, I haven't done that in a long time. Am I okay?" She looked at her hands nervously.

"We'll get an x-ray of this leg, but I think it's only bruised. You know you are almost a teenager now, and sometimes clumsiness comes with growing. Let's not draw any conclusions. Is this the first time you've lost your balance?"

"I think so. I can't remember."

"Okay, sounding pretty normal to me." He flashed a big smile. "Don't worry now. We'll get to the bottom of this. I think you've grown at least two inches since I saw you last." He knew she often became sensitive about her height, the compliment did the trick, and they rattled on a few minutes about how the school year progressed.

"Mrs. Kelly, may I speak to you in private, please." He ushered her conveniently outside the door. "I'd like to order a brain CT to make sure the tumor hasn't returned or spread, to be on the safe side."

"Yes, but you told Missy not to worry. Do you think it's returned?" She did everything she could to hold it together. It had been a grueling two years of treatment coming shortly after her divorce. The past six months felt like a haven of peace, a resemblance of normality in their lives.

"As I told your daughter, let's not assume anything at this point. I want to confirm nothing is pressing on the cerebellum, the part of the brain which controls her balance and coordination."

"Code blue, code blue, trauma unit one, ER," rang out loud and clear over the intercom. Brian groaned within himself, wrong place at the most inconvenient times. Every staff member qualifying for code assistance rushed to the room. "I'm sorry; I must go. I'll order the CT."

He walked into the area and nearly collapsed on the floor. On the gurney lay Adaline, thirty-six weeks pregnant and covered in blood. "Oh my God, what happened?" Brian asked the EMT.

"Rollover accident, they resuscitated her, but the baby's heart beat is weak." The medic replied.

"We must get her to OR now!" yelled the doctor in charge.

A faint whisper came from Adaline's lips. She reached toward where she heard Brian's voice.

"Wait," he protested. Brain moved close, put his ear to her lips, and took her trembling hand.

"Promise me, Brian, promise me. You'll take care of my baby. Promise me." Adaline's hand became limp in his.

"I will! I will! This can't be happening. It's not real. Oh my God, tell me this is a nightmare."

"We must go now; her heart rate is dropping!" the doctor yelled.

They pushed past the shocked Brian, and he collapsed in a chair. Lightening coursed through his body and stood him upright. He ran outside to the ambulance driver and grabbed his arm. "Was her husband with her? Where's Larry? Oh my God, he was. They were coming to stay with us." As realization hit, his world began to spin out of control. The attendant caught Brian as he fell to the ground.

He woke up to the Chief of the hospital standing over him. He lay on a couch in his office.

"We've called your wife to take you home," he said gently.

"What happened? Where's Larry, Adaline, and the baby? Oh my God, this can't be happening!" Brian felt as if his head would explode. His heart beat wildly. As he sat up slowly trying to process the information he had been given, he felt he would throw up.

"I'm sorry, Brian. I assume these are close friends or family?"

"My best friend! Lord, we want them. Please," he cried. "We want them."

"Brian, we'll tell you everything when Maria arrives. You need her support."

"Doctor, I know what that means. I've been here before. What happened?" he said sharply.

"From the report, a semi-trailer came into their lane. The driver swerved, lost control, and rolled over the embankment. He was thrown from the vehicle and killed instantly. It took the fire fighters two hours to pry his wife out. I'm sorry Brian; she did not make it through the surgery."

Tears streamed down Brian's face with an avalanche of emotions. It tore at the very root of his soul like the rapid flow of snow down the slopes, devastating everything in its path. Four weeks earlier, Adaline and Larry asked Brian and Maria to be this child's godparents.

Maria ran into the room. Brian threw himself into the comforting arms of his wife. They held each other and poured out grief as deep as the Grand Canyon.

The doctor looked at them with great tenderness. "Sit here." He motioned for them to take a seat on the couch. "We've taken the infant to the neonatal nursery. I want to keep him forty-eight hours and run some tests. He's a few weeks premature, but seems healthy in every way."

"The parents asked us to take custody of the child in an event something were to happen to them." The words broke as they exited his mouth.

"You'll be able to see the baby, but we need to make sure the paperwork is in order, before you can take the child when it is released," the Chief said compassionately.

Brian cleared his throat, "We've the paperwork and wishes of the parents at our home."

"Okay, I understand, but this is devastating news. You need to go home right now."

"My patients," Brian tried to persist.

The boss held his hand up before he could protest any further. "It's taken care of."

"I was really the only family Larry had, but were Adaline's parents contacted?" Brian moaned.

"Yes, they are making arrangements to fly here," the doctor responded.

"This is a horrific nightmare. Maria, tell me this isn't happening. Wake me up, please."

Brian and Maria sat in their car, numb from the news of losing two good friends. She could not put the car in gear. "We can't leave that baby all alone. He needs to be held, loved, and cared for. He's suffered a great injustice. It's not fair." Tears poured like a river from her eyes.

Brian opened the car door, went to the driver's side, opened Maria's door, and placed his hand in hers. "Father, you have never failed us, our hearts are being ripped out of our chests. Please don't fail us now. This baby needs us," he prayed.

They went back into the hospital and asked the chief if they could hold baby Joshua. He escorted them to the third floor and gave the nurses permission to band them. He sectioned off a room to allow them privacy. The nurse wheeled the little crib into the room. "There are diapers, a bottle with formula, and wipes here." She pointed to the drawers. "Take your time. What an overwhelming loss. I'm so sorry." She exited the room quickly.

Maria picked up the child and cradled him in her arms. "What if the grandparents want him?" she asked softly as she touched the baby's cheek.

"Let's pray they'll consider Adaline's wishes." Brian responded.

"I need to make arrangements for Larry and see where his body is. Will you be okay here? Where is Angel?" he asked anxiously.

"It's okay, honey. Ashley has her. I know we discussed not leaving her just yet, but it is an emergency," Maria defended.

"I know. It's okay. I'll get her. We'll come back here," Brian said.

"I called my parents and Barbie. They are on the way. Mom called Pastor Stroke."

"Okay, thank you. I love you." He kissed Maria and the baby on his head.

"Please, be safe," she pleaded.

"I will." Brian's occupation taught him to save his emotions for a later time and deal with the crisis at hand. He pulled himself together. His friend needed him in a way, Brian would never have imagined.

Alice Voyles and her husband, Melvin, have lived in Arizona for twenty plus years. Alice enjoys writing, sharing her desire for people to pursue their dreams through speaking and teaching, playing with her grandchildren, and hiking. After the inspiration of a high school creative writing course she pursued her passion by writing children's books and short stories. Alice hopes her writings will motivate readers to search for meaning beyond their circumstances—to find light in the darkness. Alice's hope is that the creative writings within these pages bring healing to the wounds of your soul.

a Book's Mind

Book One – *Stormy Garden*
and
Book Two – *Life's Oasis*
are also available for purchase on Alice's website
(alicevoylesauthor.com) or through a Book's Mind
at www.abooksmart.com.

If you have a book that you would like to publish,
contact Jenene Scott, Publisher, at A Book's Mind:
jenene@abooksmind.com.

www.abooksmind.com